diary of a 6th grade ninja 8

spirit week shenanigans

BY MARCUS EMERSON
AND NOAH CHILD

ILLUSTRATED BY DAVID LEE

EMERSON PUBLISHING HOUSE

ALSO BY MARCUS EMERSON

The Diary of a 6th Grade Ninja Series
Diary of a 6th Grade Ninja
Pirate Invasion
Rise of the Red Ninjas
A Game of Chase
Terror at the Talent Show
Buchanan Bandits
Scavengers
The Scavengers Strike Back
My Worst Frenemy

Middle School Ninja: Legacy

The Secret Agent 6th Grader Series
Secret Agent 6th Grader
Ice Cold Suckerpunch
Extra Large Soda Jerk
Selfies are Forever

Totes Sweet Hero

This one's for Charlotte and Emma...

Text copyright © 2014 by Emerson Publishing House.
Illustrations copyright © David Lee.

Emerson Publishing House

Book design by Marcus Emerson.

If you're thinking about recruiting a dinosaur as your sidekick, I'd recommend something *other* than a t-rex. I mean, yeah, they're totes one of the scariest dinosaurs that ever existed, but what science dudes don't tell you is just how insecure those things really are. We had only just reached the vampire queen's lair, and he was already looking for a mirror to fix his mask!

My name is Chase Cooper, and I'm a sixth grade ninja… trying to find the vampire queen with my t-rex sidekick.

"Seriously, broseph," Bennie, the t-rex, groaned. "Does this mask make my face look big?"

I stopped in the middle of the dark hallway, turning around and waving my torch high over my head to get a better look at Bennie's face, which was about twenty feet above the ground. "Um, I think your gigantic tyrannosaurus head makes your face look big."

"You know those are 'shopped,' right?" I said, spinning around and continuing my trek through the dark hall.

"My head does, but my heart doesn't," Bennie whispered.

You see what I mean? Insecure dinosaurs are the *worst*.

After a peaceful twenty seconds of silence, Bennie spoke again. "Soooo, you think the vampire queen has a mirror so I can check if my mask looks alright?"

"Why do you even wear a mask?" I asked, starting to feel slightly annoyed.

"Duh-doy! The same reason you wear yours! To protect my secret identity!"

For a second time, I spun around to look at Bennie because I wasn't sure if he was being serious or not. *"You're a dinosaur!"* I hissed. "I don't think a *ninja mask* is going to hide the fact that you're a *two story tall reptile!* You're also the only talking dinosaur in existence. I think it's pretty obvious who you are! But whatever, man. I'm almost a hundred percent positive that the vampire queen *doesn't* have a mirror since vampires can't see their reflections in them."

BENNIE

CHASE COOPER (ME)

"But she would probably have one for her guests, right? Like, for friends she has over for dinner? I mean, not *for* dinner, but to have dinner *with* her?"

I took a deep breath and exhaled slowly. "I don't know. We'll worry about that after we find her. You seriously need to focus – get your head back in the game!"

"Right," Bennie said, nodding his giant head once. "In the

2

game. The *zone.* The *game zone.* The *zone* where *games* are played, like, for real, yo."

A thin strip of light flickered about thirty feet in front of us. Pushing my torch into the soft dirt of the floor, I snuffed out the flame so Bennie and I were hidden in the shadows.

"There," Bennie said. "That's the door to her lair."

"Do you think she knows we're out here?" I asked, taking one step forward.

Just then, a voice hissed through the air. "I wouldn't be a very good vampire if I didn't."

"Uh-oh," I said.

"Who has come to visit me?" the voice asked out of thin air.

"It's me, Chase Cooper," I said. "I come from the land of dirty laundry and half empty soda cans, also known as my bedroom."

"*Cooper,*" the voice replied in a way that I could tell there was a wicked smile on the face of whoever was speaking.

The glowing strip at the end of the hall burst, drowning the corridor in a blinding flood of light. I squeezed my eyes shut, but the light was so intense that my eyeballs still burned behind my eyelids. Even if I *could* open my eyes, I wouldn't be able to see anything.

I heard the sound of the brick walls crumbling around Bennie and me. It was violent and deafening.

"Bennie!" I shouted over the roar of disintegrating bricks and mortar. "You still with me? You okay?"

Bennie's voice replied. "I can't cover my eyes! My tiny dinosaur arms are too short! Darn these tiny arms! Are they *too* short? Do you think they make me look weird?"

I ignored Bennie's question and pressed forward, feeling the ground rumble under my feet. The queen was playing mind games with us, and I knew it.

There *wasn't* really an explosion in front of us, and the walls *weren't* really crumbling apart. It was all in our heads, planted there by the vampire queen. "Just keep moving forward!" I shouted, keeping my eyes closed. "Get ready to charge!"

"Roger that!" Bennie said, stomping his massive legs as we prepared to storm the queen's lair.

I held my breath and tried to calm my mind, but it was

nearly impossible since we were so close to the vampire queen. "Forget this!" I said. "Just run!"

Stepping to the side, I let Bennie go first since he was the size of a house. As soon as he staggered past me, I jumped back to the center of the hallway and sprinted behind him. "Go! Just break through the door! Once we're in the same room as the vampire queen, this illusion will end!"

The t-rex roared loudly as he crashed into the wall at the end of the hallway.

And then the illusion of blinding light and melting walls disappeared, leaving Bennie and me behind in the cold air of the next room.

"Well done," the voice of the vampire queen hissed.

Dust floated slowly like it was frozen in time as I jumped to my feet, scanning the room for the most powerful enemy I'd ever encountered. Robot James Buchanan and the Ice Queen of Scrag

Seven were bad, but the vampire queen was a whole new level of crazy.

And she wasn't *only* a vampire queen. She was a *ninja* vampire queen.

Two hands gripped my shoulders from behind me and tossed me across the room like a ragdoll. I flipped in midair, barely keeping myself from squashing against the wall like a bug on a windshield.

Dropping to my feet, I had just enough time to collect myself before getting tossed across the room again by the queen.

"Chase!" Bennie shouted as he leapt toward me.

Catching his rough skin with my hands, I dug my fingers into his scales and pulled myself to safety on his back.

The vampire queen's voice sliced through the air like ninja stars. "You dare enter my home uninvited?"

Bennie stomped backward, darting his head left and right trying to find the source of the queen's voice. As a vampire, she could've been anywhere in her lair.

Suddenly, a black smoke drifted from the shadows and swirled at the spot in front of my dinosaur sidekick. I watched as the smoke formed into a solid shape on the floor. As the vapor climbed higher, it slowly morphed into a person right before my eyes.

Within seconds, the smoke fully formed into the vampire queen. A tattered purple scarf rested on her shoulders that covered the bottom half of the vampire's face.

The queen arched her neck, cracking it like she had just woken up. Her eyes met mine as she took a seat on a cracked concrete throne. Pulling one leg up, she wrapped her hands around her knee and held it in place.

"S'up," she said as if we were old friends.

Bennie didn't waste any time. The instant the queen sat, he dove forward hoping to smoosh her out of existence. His 9 ton dinosaur body tore through her concrete throne, but not before the vampire queen burst into a cloud of smoke, teleporting safely to another spot in the room. I managed to jump off my sidekick and land safely before he plowed into the wall.

"Down, boy," the queen said as she raised her open palm. An ice cream cone materialized above her hand. "Who's been a good boy?" the queen said, pressing her lips together and talking with a cute baby voice. "Who's been a good boy?"

Bennie's weakness was ice cream.

THE VAMPIRE QUEEN
(IN PROBABLY THE COOLEST CHAIR I'VE EVER SEEN!)

Rolling to his back like a dog, he wiggled both of his itty bitty stick arms like he was trying to get the queen's attention. "Me, me, me!" he giggled. "Yay, ice cream!"

The vampire queen tossed the ice cream cone through the air.

Bennie sat up and caught the treat with his small claw hand. He lifted it to his face and stuck out his tongue, trying to get a lick of the ice cream.

The thing Bennie often forgot was how almost impossible it was for him to eat an ice cream cone. His short arms kept him from ever getting a lick.

The vampire queen knew this and used it against him.

So there I was, facing the vampire queen as my dinosaur sidekick was totally distracted. At that point I was pretty much on my own. There was no way Bennie was going to take his eyes off his sweet treat.

"You got lucky with the ice cream," I said, stepping slowly around the vampire queen, keeping her a safe distance from me the entire time.

ICE CREAM + T-REX

THIS IMAGE HAS BEEN BROUGHT TO YOU BY MATH!

...NOT REALLY. IT WAS ACTUALLY BROUGHT TO YOU BY DINOSAURS, ICE CREAM CONES, AND BROKEN DREAMS.

"It wasn't luck," the queen sneered. "Don't you remember? I know *everyone's* secrets. It's my job..." she said, pausing for effect as she pulled her scarf lower, revealing the rest of her face. Then she finished her sentence, "as a *Scavenger*."

I stumbled over my feet, shocked by what I saw. I wanted to speak, but my words got lost in my throat. Standing only a few feet away from me was the vampire queen...

It was my old friend Naomi.

She flung her cape off her shoulders and strutted toward me like she was in a fashion show. "Remember when we used to be friends?" she asked, smirking. "Remember all the good times we had?"

"Remember when you betrayed me, and turned out to be one of the most monstrous villains I'd ever come across? Remember when you ruined my life by getting everyone to hate me? Remember any of *that*?"

Naomi pouted. "Kind of," she said. "I guess I remember it differently."

I knew I should've kept quiet because Naomi was trying to get me to talk. I shouldn't have responded at all, but I guess my brain wanted the opposite. I know, right? Sometimes my brain thinks it's smarter than me.

"How can you remember it differently?" I said. "Because that's exactly what happened! Our friendship *ended* in betrayal!"

Bennie looked up from his ice cream cone. "Um, what's this crazy lady talking about?"

"Doesn't he know?" Naomi asked, stepping toward me. She moved through the room like she was completely weightless. "Doesn't he know about… *us*?"

"Dude, this is getting weird," Bennie said. "Tell me what she's talking about! Did you used to go out with her?"

"No!" I snipped. "It's complicated!"

The vampire queen laughed. "It's not *that* complicated. Tell him, Chase. Tell your dinosaur sidekick how you and I used to be BFFs…"

"No way," Bennie said. "You and the vampire queen?"

I stared at Naomi as she continued her approach. "That was the past, and I didn't know she was an evil, life-sucking vampire at the time!"

"Chase," Naomi said through a soft smile. "You sadden me with your words. Remember how we used to train together? Remember when we were on the same team? We used to split our French fries at lunch!"

I squeezed my eyes shut and shook my head. "No! It wasn't real! You were playing me the whole time! You were playing *everyone!*"

Naomi's voice was right next to me. "It's not too late to join me, and you know it."

"It's never too late for *you* to stop… being a vampire!" I said defensively, fully knowing it came out less intelligent than I wanted.

The vampire queen grabbed my shoulders. "Then I guess we'll have to do this the hard way." Squeezing her hands, she yanked me closer and opened her mouth, hissing the entire time.

"*Chase!*" Bennie roared from across the room.

"*NO!*" I shouted through clenched teeth.

My legs kicked forward, and I was suddenly on my back staring at ceiling tiles. The hissing vampire queen was no longer there. Instead, I heard the sound of giggling students drift overhead.

"Great," I whispered, sitting upright, trying to focus my blurry vision on my friends as they hovered around me. It was Zoe, Gavin, Faith, and Brayden… and they were wearing their pajamas.

Monday. 11:59 AM. Back to reality.

Why were my friends dressed for a slumber party? Did I fall asleep at a sleepover or something? Where in the heck was I? Those were the questions forming in my noggin as I blinked back to life.

I glanced past my friends and saw the tinted windows of the cafeteria. Through the glass was a mess of activity as students sat at different tables eating lunch and laughing with each other.

"Oh, that's right," I said aloud, remembering that I *was* at school, and my friends were wearing pajamas because that was the Spirit Week theme of the day.

"Game over!" my phone repeated from the carpet by my feet. I snatched it up and looked at the screen. The vampire queen had killed my character, which was always what happened at the end of that game.

I guess I got too carried away in the game's story. You ever do that? Naomi and I obviously weren't characters in it, but my brain made it that way. And there wasn't actually a t-rex sidekick in the game. My imagination did that too.

There's a picture of me getting "in the zone" during an intense part of the game. Mouth open, eyelids peeled back, legs crossed because I'm about to beat a super hard part. C'mon, we're all guilty of that, right? Anyone?

The other students of Buchanan School waited patiently in

the lobby for lunch to end. A lot of them were glaring at me, but a few smiled.

Even the school janitor, Miss Chen-Jung, was giving me what looked like a pity smile. She was a short Korean woman who was on her last year at Buchanan School. I don't know how old she was, but she was retiring at the end of the school year, so I guess *that* old. How old do you have to be to retire? Like, 90?

After scarfing down my food in the cafeteria, I decided to come out to the lobby to wait until lunch was over. With the several minutes I had to try and kill, I spent it playing some cheap vampire hunting game.

"So let's see," I heard Zoe's voice say. "If the dream was about fighting other ninjas, then you had leftover pizza for breakfast. If it was about fighting a giant sized robot version of President Buchanan, then you probably ate cold hotdogs."

Finally, my eyes adjusted, but only after I rubbed them awake a little. "And what if I was fighting a vampire queen?" I asked.

Zoe hummed, placing her finger under her chin. "Hmmm, I'm thinking... leftover cake from brunch yesterday?"

My cousin was talking about the Sunday brunch our families shared together.

"Wait," Zoe said, her eyes wide open. "Was the vampire queen a *ninja* too?"

"Why's that matter?" I asked, staring at the floor.

Faith smiled as she leaned one shoulder against the wall. She snapped her finger at Zoe. "Oh, I got this! Leftover cake *and* pizza for breakfast!"

Everyone laughed, but it was cool since they were my best friends.

"Har har, guys," I said, rubbing life back into my cheeks. Pushing my phone into my front pocket, I said, "But you're all wrong. I *wasn't* asleep. I was just zoned out from playing a game on my cell. And, FYI, I had microwaved mac and cheese with awesome sauce for breakfast."

"What's awesome sauce?" Faith asked.

"It's a secret," I said.

"It's ketchup," Zoe said flatly. "All he does is squeeze ketchup over his mac and cheese. It's nasty."

Faith's smile disappeared, like, totally, as if she had just seen a train accident. *"That's the grossest thing I've ever heard,"* she whispered as her face turned white.

"Are you kidding me?" Gavin asked. "Ketchup on mac and cheese go together like sandwiches and chips! It's the food of kings!"

"Not you too!" Zoe scoffed at Gavin.

Faith gulped. "Maybe I'm just against mac and cheese because I got food poisoning from some back in fourth grade."

"Food poisoning? Did it give you superpowers?" I joked.

Faith paused. "If uncontrollable barfing is a superpower… then, yes, it gave me superpowers."

"Barfing superpowers? That would be the worst thing in the world," Brayden said. "But I'd be the first in line to see it."

I cringed at the thought of the worst superpower ever. Can you imagine? Wait, no, don't. Don't imagine *barfing on command* as a tool against evil.

I ALMOST INCLUDED AN IMAGE OF A BARFING SUPERPOWER, BUT DECIDED AGAINST IT. HERE'S A NINJA RACCOON INSTEAD. HIS NAME IS NAOKI.

Zoe's face had started to look pale from our conversation. She grabbed Gavin's hand and held it tightly as a way to comfort herself.

For those of you who are curious – my cousin and Gavin were *officially* an item. Like, girlfriend/boyfriend.

Zoe's my cousin so naturally I felt protective of her, but I also knew she was a big girl and could handle herself. "Their relationship doesn't really gross me out anymore," is what I'd say if their relationship didn't gross me out anymore, but like that one president who cut down that tree, I could not tell a lie... which meant their relationship *totally* grossed me out.

I didn't normally care about those kinds of things, but since Zoe *was* my cousin, I saw the situation a little differently.

Brayden clutched the straps of his book bag and kicked my shoe to get my attention. "You comin' then? Or are you gonna try and catch a nap?"

It wasn't a secret to anyone that I enjoyed a nap here and there... or everywhere really.

"Don't blink or you'll fall asleep," Faith said.

"Ninjas don't blink," I replied. "They have their eyelids removed at a very young age and learn to deal with dry eyes."

"Yuck," Faith said, wrinkling her nose at me.

Zoe's brow raised, concerned. "You should really get more sleep at night."

"A ninja never stops training," I said, standing to my feet, but taking an extra second to walk because I felt dizzy.

"Right, training," Zoe replied, making air quotes with her fingers. "You mean video games or late night horror movie marathons."

Gavin shook his head. "I dunno how you can watch that stuff at night," he said with his Texan accent. Gavin had moved to the area from Texas awhile back. "Them movies scare the hair off a m'legs."

"Thank you for that *lovely* imagery," Faith groaned. "Thousands of little hairs jumping off your skinny legs and running for their lives."

"You mean *dozens* of little hairs, right?" I joked.

Everyone laughed.

"It ain't my fault I got smooth ladylike legs!" Gavin said through a smile. "I'll make a good swimmer someday!"

"But until then," Zoe said, joining the pile on, "you'll make a good model for capri pants."

Gavin checked his watch, and then spoke to my cousin. "You'd better get going," he said, worried. "You've only got a few minutes until the assembly."

"Oh, thanks!" Zoe said, turning her slow walk into a speed walk complete with locked elbows and everything. About ten feet down the hall, she shouted over her shoulder. "See you guys in the gym!"

"You coming too?" Brayden asked me again.

I nodded. "Yeah, I'll catch up. Save me a seat, okay?"

"Got it," Brayden said, bumping his fist against mine.

Stretching my back, I waited for another second before leaving the lobby. The bell was going to ring at any moment, and I wanted to see if I could catch Melvin before he went into the Spirit Week assembly.

For anyone just joining our program, let me fill you in on the crazy details of my life since my last "chronicle" entry…

My cousin Zoe, the girl who had given me a hard time only moments ago, was the new president of Buchanan School. She had earned the position last Friday, which was only three days ago.

Basically, it's only been a weekend since Zoe won the presidency, and Principal Davis wanted to kick off her term with a bang.

Buchanan School had been through a lot over the past few weeks starting with a scandal that involved Sebastian, the previous president, and ending with a rigged election that had been uncovered by a student reporter named Melvin.

Spirit Week was Principal Davis's way of trying to get a pulse back into the veins of Buchanan School. And honestly, with everything that's happened, it was a great idea.

Zoe was so excited about it that it was all she talked about over the entire weekend.

My phone buzzed every ten minutes with a text message from her about a fun idea she had or a great way to raise money for different school clubs.

I didn't mind the messages at all. In fact, I was happy to see they were from her because every time my phone vibrated, my heart skipped a beat because I was afraid it was going to be Naomi.

She used to be one of the best ninjas in my ninja clan. She also used to be one of my best friends. I say "used to be" because just last week she revealed herself as the leader of a dangerous group of students at Buchanan called The Scavengers.

I thought that a scavenger was just an animal that feeds on other dead animals, but the Internet also defines it as someone who collects discarded material, which is exactly what Naomi's Scavengers do.

The group is made up of several kids and always operates in the background, listening and collecting gossip. They're never seen nor heard, and the group is so secret that it's a mystery as to who's actually part of their club.

Their main source of information is from the notes that students toss in the garbage. Ever write a note to someone in school? Well, at Buchanan School, when that note is thrown away, a Scavenger plucks it from the trashcan and documents every juicy little nugget of gossip that was in it.

You think your crush is just between you and your BFF? If you go to my school, you'd better believe it's not. I don't know about you, but I've thrown about a billion notes away in the trash.

The craziest part though is that The Scavengers are a group that's been around since the school was first built about a hundred years ago. That's right, they've operated in the shadows since the beginning, and Naomi was just another leader on their list.

Every president at Buchanan had been a Scavenger, which was exactly how they got into that position. Scavengers controlled everything and nobody had a clue they even existed.

In fact, a Scavenger would still be the president of the school if it weren't for the quick thinking of a student reporter named Melvin.

Zoe's the first president ever that *wasn't* a Scavenger, but even she had no clue about them. And that's what scared me... what was Naomi planning on doing about it? Hopefully nothing, but if you're at all familiar with my life then you know that it's *never* nothing.

Naomi was part of my ninja clan since the second week of school, but even at that time, she was just a spy. The Scavengers are like the ninjas to other ninjas.

So last week, I stumbled upon Naomi's secret. And she didn't try hiding it or playing it off either – she came right out and told me she was their leader. She was like, "Oh, BTW, I'm the leader of a terrifying group of kids at this school. K, bye!"

Here's the part that confuses me to my core though – Naomi turned out to be the bad girl, but it broke my heart… and I miss her friendship so much that it kills me. Pretty sappy, right? Well, that's how I felt, and I'm not gonna lie about it.

The Scavengers also asked me to join their group earlier that week, before I knew Naomi was their leader. Obviously I told them to bug off, and that's what set a whole different machine in motion.

After that, my life slowly started falling apart from a carefully planned plot. I won't go too much into it, but let's just say it was seriously my roughest week at Buchanan School.

I lost friends and made new enemies without even lifting a finger! The Scavengers had planned their attack so carefully that it was possible that a lot of kids were going to hate me for the rest of their lives.

The Scavengers put out a paper called The Chase Cooper Newsletter of Secrets, which was *filled* with gossip about students that would make their parents cry.

But that's not all… besides Brayden, every ninja in my clan quit and joined the Scavengers. It wasn't much of a jump for them since they found out Naomi led the group.

I'm not sure why, but ever since I was put in charge of the ninja clan at the beginning of the school year, I'd had trouble keeping it together. I'm not exactly sure why everyone kept quitting, but I was beginning to think it's because I'm not that good of a leader. Bummer, right?

So far, only a handful of people knew I wasn't the one behind the newsletter, and that was on purpose. I was still trying to figure out the best course of action to take with it. If I went to the principal, then I'd have to tell him about Naomi and the Scavengers, which meant that my secret of having a ninja clan would also come out.

But it was mostly because of Zoe that I hadn't told anyone about the Scavengers yet. She was so excited about winning the presidency that I didn't want to burst her bubble with another bizarre situation.

Which brings us back to the present – back to me standing in the lobby of Buchanan School waiting to see if I could find

Melvin before the assembly.

    I kept my eyes focused on the floor, only glancing up a few times to see if Melvin was around. Everyone in the school hated me so I was worried that if I made eye contact with the wrong kid, it would mean getting shoulder-checked into the wall.

    Luckily, I never got checked, but I got more stink-eyes than you could shake a stick at. That's if you were into shaking sticks, but you've probably got better things to do with your time, right? I'm sorry, but does anybody actually shake sticks at things? Like, who does that? Ugh, nevermind.

    At that moment, the bell rang loudly over my head.

    Students began flooding the halls of the school, shuffling their feet across the carpeted floor like zombies in a parade, making their way to the gymnasium.

    And I also never saw Melvin. No biggie though. I would just have to catch up with him during our ninja training later on.

Monday. 12:10 PM. The gymnasium.

About ten minutes later, I stepped into the gym somewhat late for the assembly. I lagged behind hoping all the seats would be taken so I'd have to stand at the side of the bleachers. Too bad my homeroom teacher, Mrs. Robinson, was standing by the door; she wasn't about to let me hide in the dark.

Principal Davis was already speaking into the microphone, thanking everyone for attending the assembly that we had no other choice but to attend.

"There's an open spot right when you walk in," Mrs. Robinson said, putting her hand on my shoulder and guiding me through the entryway.

Great, I thought. Knowing my luck, I was going to get seated next to some bruiser who punches faces for fun.

"There's a spot next to Faith," Mrs. Robinson said as she nudged me around the corner.

"There you are!" Faith whispered.

When I saw her, I relaxed a little. "Hey," I replied.

Faith patted the open spot next to her. "Pull up a chair, er, *bench* or whatever. You told us to save you a seat!"

"Oh, right. You guys saved me a seat," I chuckled, but nobody could hear it since the principal was in the middle of his welcome. Taking the spot next to Faith, I leaned forward to see who else was in our row.

Gavin and Brayden were on the other side of Faith. Last on the bench, on the other side of Brayden, was a girl I recognized, but didn't know her name. Every few seconds, Brayden would lean over to her and whisper something that made her giggle.

I was about to ask Faith who the new girl was when everyone in the gym started cheering loudly.

Zoe's voice came through the speaker system. She stood in front of the podium and addressed the school as the new president.

"Sixth graders of Buchanan School!" she said loudly. "I'd like to start off by saying thanks once again for electing me as your new president, but I'd also like to remind you that I'm planning on making my term the most *epic* term that this school has ever seen! James Buchanan will be rolling in his grave by the end of this school year!"

Everyone cheered, including me. Zoe was definitely the best choice for president. She wasn't exactly the quietest girl in the world, but she surprised me at how good she was at giving speeches in front of hundreds of kids.

"As you know, this is Spirit Week," my cousin continued. "But what does that mean? Those are just two words, right? *What* does it mean? Does it mean we're gonna dress funny everyday? Does it mean we're gonna have assemblies during the week that'll get us out of our classes? Does it mean we're gonna have team-based competitions? Snacks on the track? Couches during lunch? Ice cream during assemblies?"

The gym full of kids fell quiet, waiting for Zoe to answer her own questions. I knew she was pausing to build some tension. Everyone was on the edge of their seats waiting for something they could scream their heads off about.

And Zoe delivered. "Yes!" she said, slamming her fist into the podium. "Yes, to all those things!"

Goosebumps raised on my arms, but the good kind where I was excited and blown away.

Zoe kept going with a smile so huge that I was worried the top of her head would fall off. "This is Spirit Week, people! It's not a week for the faint of heart! It's not a week for those who like peace and quiet!" she said, and then switched her tone to a more serious one as she leaned closer to the mic. "I'd like to just warn the staff ahead of time that if you have a heart condition, maybe it's best to take this week off. And also, if you're pregnant, maybe you should refrain from teaching classes…" she paused, "because this week will rock the baby right out of you!"

All the students in the gym laughed. So did the staff, which was definitely a sign that Zoe was killing it on the microphone.

My cousin straightened out and spoke strongly again. "We're gonna have games! We're gonna have prizes! We're gonna have school wide assemblies *just* to get us out of our classes! Who *doesn't* want that?"

It was a rhetorical question, the kind that's asked but doesn't need to be answered. A few kids were still new to that concept and shouted, "We want that! We want that!"

"Buchanan School has seen a lot, and I'm only talking about *this* school year!" Zoe said. "The sixth graders here are *good* kids! And we need to remember that! It's so easy to get dragged down so this is the week where we lift each other up. *Who's with me?*"

For a third time, everyone shouted and clapped their hands. A lot of students stood to their feet, pumping their fists in the air.

"And we're starting with this assembly today!" Zoe said as she extended her arm toward the gym doors.

The doors swung open, and five guys dressed in white peddled in on bicycles. On the front of their bikes were giant boxes with pictures of ice cream cones.

"No stinkin' way," Faith whispered. "Your cousin is easily the coolest kid in the school. There's no such thing as 'over the top' with her. If it's *not* 'over the top,' then it's not Zoe."

"I know, right?" I said, remembering the t-rex sidekick from my game. "Bennie's eyes would pop out of his head if he were here."

"Who's Bennie?" Faith asked, staring at the ice cream vendors as they circled the floor of the gym.

"Uh," I said. "Nevermind."

Faith turned back to me, still holding her smile. "You know she wouldn't have any of this if it weren't for you though, right?"

"Nah," I said, blushing. "She'd be exactly where she was."

The ice cream vendors stopped their bikes behind my cousin at the podium.

Zoe continued her speech. "But before these guys start handing out ice cream, I have one more thing to say."

21

The gym full of kids fell silent, waiting for their president to continue.

"Spirit Week is also a week of competition," Zoe said. "So Principal Davis and I would like to announce the Buchanan Games! Starting tomorrow, each day will have a competition in which teams of students will participate. There will be four games total and the last team standing on Friday will be the winners! Sign ups will take place at the table in front of the gym right after I wrap up talking. Now here's the best part…" Zoe said, as she glanced at Principal Davis.

The principal nodded, giving her the thumbs-up to go ahead and make another announcement.

Zoe smiled. "The *winners* of the competition will be allowed to start whatever club they want that will be officially recognized by the school. Your club photo will be in the yearbook and everything."

The applause was loud, but not as big that time.

"Oh, and did I mention," Zoe said, "that the winning team will also be given a budget of a thousand dollars? The staff of Buchanan School has moved some money around so that the new club gets that extra special 'oomph' it needs to start up."

That was what the students needed to hear to explode with another set of cheers, and who could blame them? A thousand bucks is a *ton* of money for any club! Could you imagine what I could do if my ninja clan had a *thousand* dollars to spend on supplies?

I mean, if I even had a ninja clan to lead anymore.

Monday. 12:30 PM. The gymnasium.

Zoe wrapped up her speech and invited all the sixth graders to the floor of the gymnasium to grab a free ice cream cone from one of the vendors. I stayed close to my friends because I didn't want to get caught sitting alone.

"One chocolate please," I said to the older dude on the bike.

"Not a problem," he said, reaching his hand into the portable freezer. "That'll be two bucks."

I froze as I held my hand out to get the ice cream cone he was holding. "Oh, I thought... uh..."

"I'm kidding," the man laughed, handing me the cone. "Now get outta here, I got other customers, y'know!"

My friends laughed from behind me. They had already gotten their ice cream and had taken the wrapping off the tops.

"Funny," I said, just a little embarrassed. Taking the top piece of paper off my cone, I tossed it into one of the trashcans that had been wheeled in from the cafeteria.

"Zoe's makin' a name for herself pretty quickly," Gavin said. "This is the sorta thing that'll be talked about for years to come."

"Right?" Faith asked, taking a chomp out of her cone. She looked at me with a mouthful of strawberry ice cream. "You got your work cut out for ya."

I was about to take a lick of my own ice cream, but stopped. "Me? Why?"

Faith shrugged her shoulder. "I'unno," she mumbled. "I just thought maybe you wouldn't want to live in her shadow the whole time?"

With a smile, I leaned closer. "I think we *both* know a little something about living in the shadows, am I right?"

Faith looked at me confused. "Huh?" she grunted, taking another huge bite of ice cream. "What are you talking about? And why are you leaning closer to me like a creep?"

My eyes narrowed as I froze in place, still leaning. "I'm just... I mean... um..."

I was referring to the white ninja that had appeared to me a few times before in the year. Twice, the white ninja saved me from trouble, but both times I barely got to speak a word to the masked vigilante.

However, last week Faith had hinted at the fact that *she* was the white ninja, but her weird response at that moment made me question if I had heard her correctly.

"But you said..." I continued, dragging out the sentence.

My hope was that Faith would try to interrupt me so her secret would be safe from Brayden and Gavin, but instead, she lifted her chin and said, "Go on. What did I say?"

"Yeah, dude," Gavin said. "What'd Faith say?"

I tightened a smile and stared at my ice cream cone.

"Nothing," I said. I was so confused and didn't want to say something stupid. "She never said anything to me."

How frustrating! *Was* Faith the white ninja? Was she *not*? If she *was* then why was she acting clueless? I decided to drop the subject. I'm sure time would tell if she *was* or *wasn't* the secret white ninja.

"So are you guys gonna compete in the games this week?" I asked.

"I think you can only compete if you're on a team," Brayden said. He pointed at me. "Hey, wanna team up? Do you guys want to be on a team?"

Faith nodded, smiling.

"Why not?" Gavin said, cracking a smile with the side of his mouth.

I paused. "Y'know," I said. "I think I'm going to sit this one out. I feel like I've been on my toes since the first day of school. I'd like to just hang out this time."

Everyone grumbled, but agreed with me the way friends do when they're not really agreeing with you.

"Besides, I'm pretty sure everyone still hates me because of last week," I added.

Brayden and Melvin were the only people who knew that it wasn't *me* who put out the Chase Cooper Newsletter of Secrets. I never said anything to Gavin, Zoe, or Faith about it, but I kind of think they suspected there was something more going on than anyone realized. I was glad they didn't push the matter.

Still staring at my ice cream cone, I noticed that it was beginning to melt down the sides and onto my hand. I would've licked it up, but I was all too aware that my friends were still watching me so I didn't do anything.

"You gonna get that?" Gavin asked.

"When I'm ready," I said, watching more of the ice cream melt.

"Like, soon? Because it's kind of getting everywhere."

Here's a little something about me – I get kind of shy when I know people are watching me or waiting for me to do something. At that moment, I didn't want to lick the ice cream since I was the center of attention. I wasn't about to lick my ice cream while keeping eye contact with any of my friends. If that's not the creepiest thing to do in the world, then I don't know what is.

"This is painful to watch," Faith said.

"That's the point!" I replied. "I'd be fine if you guys weren't *watching* me right now!"

Just then, a girl hopped up to us. It was the same girl that Brayden had been sitting next to during the assembly. She was sporting a bright smile until she saw the ice cream all over my hand. "OMG, why aren't you eating that? It's getting *everywhere!*"

"I'm gettin' there!" I said. "Wait, who are you?"

Brayden stepped forward. "Guys, this is Danielle Jenkins," he said, and then he leaned closer to me as he wiped his mouth, and whispered, "Dude, do I got any ice cream on my face?"

"Not on the outside," I said, a little too proud of my lame joke.

"On the inside?" Brayden whispered sarcastically and a little annoyed. "There's ice cream on the inside of my face?"

"Uhg," Danielle groaned, tilting her head back. "Brayden, call me *Dani*. I hate when people call me Danielle. It sounds like such a kindergartner's name."

"Sorry," he said. "Guys, this is *Dani* Jenkins, my friend."

"*Ohhhhhhh!*" Gavin hollered. "*Bray-den's got a girl-friend! Bray-den's got a girl-friend!*"

Brayden's face turned serious. "Really?"

Gavin stopped, but still kept his grin.

"Hey, Dani," I said, trying to make the awkward silence go away. "Whuddup?"

"Not much," she said.

"Dani's on the student council with Zoe," Brayden bragged.

"It's not that big of a deal," Dani said. "I'm just the student council secretary, so all I do is take notes during meetings and stuff."

"Don't play it down," Brayden said. "What you do is important!"

"I guess," Dani said, blushing. "I mean, I do *more* than *just take notes*. I only say that 'cause I don't like talking about myself."

"You're not *that* important," another student said, almost appearing out of nowhere, standing on the other side of me. He pointed at the liquid chocolate that was pooled inside my ice cream cone. "You got a little somethin' on your hand."

My shoulders sunk. My whole frozen treat was ruined all because it was too weird to eat in front of people. "*I know,*" I said.

Brayden came to Dani's defense. "Who are you to say she's not important?"

"Easy, tiger," the boy said. "I was only joking."

Dani stepped forward. "This is Colin," she said, and then pointed to another boy standing nearby who was watching us, almost like he was alien studying a herd of humans. "And that guy creepin' back there is Bounty."

"Like the paper towel?" I asked.

"Like the hunter!" Bounty said loudly. "The way cool hunter who travels the galaxy!"

"But also dies because he tripped into the Sarlacc pit!" I scoffed.

Suddenly, Bounty was right by my side as if he teleported there. "He didn't die in that pit! He managed to escape, which means he's the toughest bounty hunter there is!"

Faith stared at Bounty and me, baffled. "I'm not exactly sure what the two of you are talking about, but I have a feeling that you guys just set off a nerd alarm somewhere in the world."

"Whatever!" I said to Faith. "You totally know what we're talking about!"

Faith kept a straight face for about a second and a half. Then she giggled. "Yeah, you're right. Those movies are pretty awesome."

"Ohhh," Gavin said, shaking his head. "I can honestly say I don't have a clue about what you guys are talking about."

"Do you ever?" Faith joked.

Gavin gave a fake smile.

Dani pointed at the two boys who had nudged their way into our circle. "These guys are also on the student council with Zoe and me. Colin's the treasurer, and Bounty's the public relations director."

"No vice president?" Faith asked.

"Not this time around," Dani explained. "Principal Davis was thinking about letting Zoe handpick a vice president since the *last* one didn't fare too well."

She was talking about Wyatt.

Let me tell you a little bit about the kid who seems to have it out for me. Wyatt is a short kid with a tall ego. He *used* to be the vice president of Buchanan, but after it was discovered that he had a hand in Sebastian's scandal, that changed.

Wyatt wasn't fired or anything, but Principal Davis rebooted the whole system since it was rotten from the inside out.

Wyatt's also the leader of the red ninja clan, which he created after I took control of his old one. The red ninjas have been training in secret in the abandoned greenhouse at the center of the school. They've been recruiting members like crazy over the past few months, and I'm not exactly sure why. It's almost as if Wyatt was creating an army. But for what? I don't know.

I have a feeling that when I'm ninety years old, Wyatt will still lurk in the background of my life spitting wads of paper at me through a straw.

28

"Hey, Dani, we should prob'ly bounce, right?" Colin asked. He had an odd way about him, almost like he was hiding something even though he had no reason to since none of us knew who he was. And then it occurred to me that this kid might hate me for the newsletter I had supposedly put out a week ago.

Dani turned to Brayden. "I got a lot of work to do," she said. "I'll catch you after school, okay?"

Brayden's eyes softened as his body melted a little. "Sure," he sighed.

Barf.

Suddenly, Zoe crashed into me from behind. I had to stumble forward to keep from falling over.

"What gives?" I asked.

She looked panicked as she caught her breath. "It's… it's…"

"The zombie invasion has started, hasn't it?" Faith asked.

My cousin lifted a sheet of paper, jabbing at it with her finger. "Wyatt," she said. "It's Wyatt. He signed up for the competition."

"So?" I asked. "That doesn't surprise me."

Zoe stopped and focused her eyes on my hand with the melted ice cream. "You know you were supposed to *eat* that, right?"

"Gah!" I grunted, frustrated. And then I marched to the nearest trashcan about ten feet away and dumped the cone into it. "Is everyone happy now?" I asked as I wiped my hands clean with a napkin I took from the same garbage can. Don't judge me.

Zoe continued. "So you know how the winning team gets to create a club that'll be recognized as an 'official' club of Buchanan?"

I nodded slowly, connecting the dots in my head. "No way," I said. "There's no way Wyatt would be *that* bold."

Zoe pushed her lips to one side of her face and nodded back at me. "As part of the registration, students had to fill out a section describing what kind of club they'd start if they won."

"And Wyatt put down 'ninja clan,' didn't he?" I asked, already knowing the answer.

Again, Zoe nodded.

"Why would he do that?" Brayden asked. "He's already got

a ninja clan."

"I know," Zoe said, finally having caught her breath. "But don't you see what he's doing?"

"Um, no?" Brayden said.

"Then allow me to explain," came a voice from outside our circle. Before I turned to look, I already knew it was Wyatt. "I'm sure by now Zoe's opened her big mouth and blabbed about the fact that I filled out the 'club' section of the registration with my desire to create a ninja clan."

"Where's your girlfriend?" Faith asked.

Faith was talking about a girl named Olivia Jones. Olive and Wyatt had been going out for the past few months. He was never without her, which was why it was a little weird that she wasn't there.

Wyatt flinched. "Things are complicated between us right now."

"Oh yeah?" Faith said. "Does that mean she dumped you?"

I saw Wyatt's jaw muscles twitch. "No," he replied. "It means it's nunya."

Faith cracked a sly smile.

"But why start a public ninja club?" Brayden asked.

Before Wyatt spoke, I already knew what his answer was going to be.

"Because," Wyatt said, "My ninja clan won't have to train in secret anymore. We'll be able to train right out in the open. We'll be able to do whatever we want since we'll be an official club in the school. I'll operate the red ninjas right under the principal's nose, and there's not a thing he can do to stop me! As a matter of fact, he's going to *give* us a thousand dollars to spend on gear! Can you imagine what I could do if my ninja clan had a *thousand* dollars to spend on supplies?"

I bit the inside of my cheek. I hated the fact that Wyatt just asked the same question that I had earlier.

Wyatt chuckled, amused by his own thoughts. "My ninja clan is going to be so *sweet*," he said, and then he looked at me. "I guess we know who the *better* leader is between the two of us."

I wanted to say something witty, but couldn't think of something fast enough. "Blah," I said under my breath. Good one, right?

Zoe scanned the paper she was holding. "It says that Jake is also competing with a team of his own."

"So?" Wyatt asked.

"Soooo…" Zoe sang. "Doesn't it bother you that he's running *against* you? Or wait," Zoe stopped, snapping her finger. "If he's just running because you want him to lose on purpose, then that's cheating. I'll have both of your teams booted from the games faster that you can say 'kitten on a kite!'"

"Kitten on a—" Wyatt whispered, a little confused. "I've *never* in my whole life heard that saying before."

"It's a real saying!" Zoe said, her cheeks flushing with red. Sometimes my cousin makes up weird phrases when her blood gets pumping.

Wyatt shrugged. "Whatever. I guess it's just a good thing that Jake isn't part of my… *club*, anymore."

Wyatt was referring to the fact that Jake was a member of his red ninja clan. Er, *used* to be a member. During election week, Jake pulled my ninja mask off my face, exposing my identity to Melvin – something I knew Wyatt would be against. Wyatt didn't

31

follow much of a code of honor, except when it came to our identities.

Everyone in our small huddle knew that I was a ninja and that Wyatt was the leader of his own clan of ninjas, which was why he was speaking so freely about it.

Wyatt looked right at me. "Jake crossed the line," he said, but that was it. He didn't explain himself or say anything else.

He was talking about Jake unmasking me. On one hand, it was cool. On the other hand, Jake was probably going to have a huge grudge against me because of it. Add that to the list of things that'll give me an ulcer, I guess.

Wyatt nodded his head once, and then walked away.

Faith looked confused. "I'm not sure whether Wyatt is a good villain or bad. Would a good villain monologue his entire plan to their enemy?"

"His ego is bigger than his head," Zoe said. "He's just so sure of himself."

"That's what it is though, right?" I said. "He's so sure he's going to win that it doesn't matter if we know his plan or not. He's basically bragging about his victory before it even happens."

Zoe held up Wyatt's registration papers again, but slid a blank one out from behind them. "Which is why you're going to participate in these games," she said, basically ordering me to compete.

Faith lifted her hands to her mouth, hiding a smile as her eyes lit up. "Oh!"

I sighed, taking the blank forms from my cousin.

Honestly, I really wanted to disappear in the background for awhile as the whole newsletter debacle died down. The last thing I wanted was to be the center of anyone's attention, especially competing in front of the entire school.

But because of Wyatt entering the competition, I knew I couldn't just sit around and do nothing. It's pretty safe to say that Wyatt winning the games and getting an official club of his own for his ninja crew was not only bad news for me, but also bad news for Buchanan School.

A small part of me even felt that Wyatt's victory in the games would've somehow been bad news for all of humanity too, but that's almost *too* epic, right?

Monday. 12:50 PM. The wrestling room.

Because of the assembly, classes for the rest of the day were shortened so school could still dismiss on time, which meant that my science class wasn't going to start until one-o-clock.

After I saw that it was ten 'til, I rushed out of the assembly and headed straight for the wrestling room. It was the first day of training with my new ninja clan, and I was already behind schedule.

A few months ago, during the week of the talent show, I stumbled upon a second gymnasium that wasn't being used. It was the wrestling room. Coach Cooper, the gym teacher (same last name as me, but not related... or *is* he? *Dun dun dunnnnnnn...* no, I'm kidding. We're not related), said that Buchanan School used to have a wrestling team, but cut it from the program because of money issues about ten years back. I asked if it was cool that I used the room for a martial arts club, and he said yeah.

I had lost every member in my ninja clan except for Brayden, so membership was at an all time low, which bummed me out more than I'd like to admit.

But I didn't want to let that ruin my year so rather than focusing on *losing* members, I was trying to be positive and see this as a new challenge for *adding* members.

All I wanted since the beginning of the school year was to be a good leader, so I saw this as a second chance at being just that.

And it would've been great, had I not been twenty minutes late to our first meeting.

Melvin was standing with his arms crossed when I entered the wrestling room. He was a reporter for the school newspaper, and the same kid who busted the lid off the rigged election a week ago. I thought he'd make a good ninja since he had all sorts of connections with other students from being a reporter.

"This is part of the lesson, right?" Melvin asked, clearly annoyed. "Like, you're showing us how you've actually been here the entire time, but hidden in the shadows, correct?"

I put my hand on my chest, feeling my heart race as I took a couple deep breaths so I wasn't wheezing when I answered. "Sorry, guys," I said. "Some stuff came up during the assembly and I just lost track of the time."

Leaning against the wall was a girl with her face hidden from view because she was staring into a cellphone, tapping furiously at the screen with her thumbs. Next to her was a boy, sitting with his legs crossed, slouching over and drawing pictures in the dust on the wrestling mat. They were two of Melvin's friends that he asked to come because he thought they'd fit well in the ninja clan.

"You're twenty minutes late," the girl said coldly, without taking her attention away from her cellphone. "I missed out on the ice cream because of this."

"Yeah, sorry," I said. "It won't happen again."

The girl looked up from her device. She was wearing a mask, but just over her eyes. It was the kind of mask that superhero sidekicks wore. "Better not."

"What's on your face?" I asked, stepping in the room.

"It's my ninja mask," the girl answered, raising her eyebrows at me like it should've been obvious.

"No," I said. "That's the *opposite* of a ninja mask. A ninja mask only has a hole for your eyes. Your mask is *only* covering your eyes."

"I know," she said. "Because I'm not about to mess up my hair by pulling a black sock over my head. Who made the rules to how a ninja mask should look anyway?"

"*Ninjas*, maybe?" I said.

34

Melvin tightened a smile as he approached me. "Don't mind her attitude," he said. "It's not really attitude. Gidget just has a strong personality. She's not really arguing with you."

"Gidget?" I repeated.

The girl looked up from her cellphone finally. "You got a problem with my name?"

"Is that your real name?" I asked.

"Real enough," she replied, returning her attention to her phone.

The boy next to her jumped up, his face beaming with a smile. "And I'm Slug."

I paused for a moment, staring at the boy called Slug, unsure of how to respond.

GIDGET & SLUG
TWINS
(NOT IDENTICAL, OBVI)

TIKA TIKA TIKA TIKA

"That's not *my* real name, of course," Slug said as he rocked back and forth. "My sister started calling me that because she thought I moved as slow as a slug, but that was when we were younger, and you know how nicknames can stick with a kid

35

through the years."

"Oh, cool," I said. "So you're okay with me calling you 'Slug?'"

"Yepper pepper," he replied, leaning back and stretching his shoulders out. I thought it was odd how he said "yepper pepper," but whatever. I ain't one to judge.

"Your sister sounds like a nimrod though," I added, trying to be funny.

Slug stopped smiling instantly. "Dude," he whispered as he nudged his head toward Gidget. "Not cool, man. My sister's right there."

Gidget lowered her phone and stared at me through the eyeholes on her mask.

"They're twins," Melvin said, leaning toward me.

Embarrassed, I tried to cover for myself. "No! I meant nimrod in the good way!"

"What way is that?" Gidget asked.

"In Iceland, the word 'nimrod' means, um… a skilled hunter," I said. Lowering my gaze, I scratched at the back of my head. "Y'know, come to think it, that might actually be true." I jabbed my finger repeatedly against Slug's head and looked at Gidget. "Can you feel that? Because, y'know… twins?"

Gidget rolled her eyes and brought her phone back to her face. She grunted. "*So* immature. I really need to start hanging out with people my own age. I just feel like I'm *so old* around you guys."

"Dude," Slug sighed. "You're, like, *a minute and a half* older than me."

Gidget made a duck face and wobbled her head back and forth like she was silently mocking her younger twin brother.

Slug rolled his shoulders, loosening his muscles. "So when do we get to start punching things? I like punching things – walls, wooden boards, trees, toast."

"You punch toast?" I asked.

"Heck yeah!" Slug said with a hearty laugh. "Have you ever punched toast before? It pretty much *explodes* when your fist makes contact! It's crazy!"

It was beginning to look like rebuilding my ninja clan was going to be tougher than I thought.

"No," I said. "We won't be punching toast in here."

Melvin squinted at the clock on the wall. "What exactly *will* we be doing?"

"Training," I said. "Learning about honor and nobility and stuff."

"And what kind of actual ninjutsu training do you have?" Melvin asked.

"Well, besides the fact that I was born into a ninja family, I also trained for many years with shaolin monks in Japan."

"Really?" Slug asked as his jaw dropped.

I laughed. "No, not really."

"Oh, sooooo..." Melvin said, still waiting for my answer.

"Training, yes!" I said. "Mostly internet. A few ninja flicks from the 70's, but *mostly* internet."

Melvin continued to stare at me. His face was hard to read. I couldn't tell whether he was excited or disappointed.

"*Awkwaaaaaard...*" Gidget sang, staring at the face of her phone still.

Finally Slug broke the silence. "When's snack time? I'm just asking because whatever the snacks are, they have to be 100% organic, like, you better have milked the cow yourself if milk is what we're drinking."

I laughed, and then made a sarcastic joke. "Right? I milked *all* the cows for the yogurt we'll be eating later."

"Wait... yogurt's made from *milk?*" Slug said, slapping his forehead like he was worried. "My entire life has been a lie."

I laughed, but then realized that he might not have been joking.

"I'm gluten free," Gidget added from behind her phone.

The bell starting ringing in the hallway. Without looking away from her text messages, Gidget walked toward the exit with Slug and Melvin trailing behind her.

Sighing, I watched them leave.

Yup. This might not have been the best idea I'd ever had.

Tuesday. 7:30 AM. The halls of Buchanan School.

I got to school the next morning about fifteen minutes
before homeroom. I actually woke up at a decent time so I figured
I'd try to get some breakfast. On Tuesdays, the cafeteria serves
bacon, egg, and cheese croissants with a side of those hockey puck
shaped tots.

But the second I stepped into the lobby, I wondered if I was
having another one of my bizarre dreams.

"Move it or lose it," a student said to me. I couldn't tell if it
was a boy or a girl because they had an enormous alien head on
their shoulders.

I stepped aside, staring at the strange looking monster as it
passed by. When I looked down the halls of the school, I saw that
several other kids had supersized heads of other creatures too. The
heads swayed back and forth as they lumbered across the lobby.

"What in the heck?" I whispered.

"Chase Cooper! Take me to your leader!" someone behind
me said.

I turned to look, absolutely terrified at what I saw. It
sounded like Brayden's voice, but it was a gigantic kitten face that
was staring back at me.

My throat choked out a high-pitched squeal as I jumped
back.

The kitten with Brayden's voice stepped forward and sounded concerned as he reached for me. "Dude, it's cool! It's me!"

As I stepped farther back, I noticed a long banner hanging from the cafeteria windows. I breathed a sigh of relief. "Oh, right. I forgot it was Spirit Week."

THIS... IS WHAT PURE EVIL PROB'LY LOOKS LIKE.

Removing the giant kitten head from his shoulders, Brayden let out a sigh. He was sweating like he had just finished running the mile in gym. "I don't think I can wear this thing longer than five minutes," he said, wiping his brow. "Unless I want to sit in a puddle of sweat all day."

"But you could fall asleep in there, and no one would know!" I joked.

The gears started churning in Brayden's brain. I could tell because of the way he stared off into space with a hint of a grin. Slowly, without breaking eye contact with me, he put the giant kitten mask back on, took one step to the side, and then waddled down the hall.

I checked the line for breakfast, which wasn't too long. I got this thing where if I see that a line has more than ten people in it, I'll just decide not to join in. Luckily it was pretty short because I was hungrier than a… whatever is known for being hungry, I guess.

But before I could take a spot in line, my cousin came out from the front offices and stopped me. "Chase, wait!" she said, holding out her hand as if she wanted me to give her something. "Did you fill out those papers for the competition?"

"Oh, right," I said, pulling my book bag off my shoulders. Unzipping the bag, I searched inside. My textbooks were always stuffed down the back so that my bag sits properly when I wear it, but the rest of my stuff was just jam-packed into whatever bit of space I could find. It looked like a brick of smashed paper was stuffed into my bag.

Zoe sighed. She was such a neat freak that seeing my

cluttered bag was enough to send her heart racing. "You should let me clean that out for you," she said as she pulled back the opening of my canvas book bag with her finger. "Seriously, I see stuff in there from the food drive we had during the first week of school."

"It's my bag of memories!" I said, yanking out a stapled set of papers. There was a weird circle shaped stain at the bottom of the first page, like someone had set their coffee mug on it.

"Gross," Zoe said, pinching the registration form between two fingers. "You couldn't set your drink somewhere else?"

I laughed. "The *really* gross thing is that I filled that out right after you gave it to me yesterday. It hasn't left my bag the entire time since then!"

Zoe's face flushed white. "Something in your bag is leaking, and you need to get it taken care of."

"Meh," I said, stretching my back and cracking it while keeping an eye on the breakfast line. A few other kids had joined it, but it was still short enough for me to jump into.

My cousin scanned through the registration form. Her eyes darted back and forth as she read what I had filled out. "Wait," she said. "It says here Brayden, Faith, and Gavin are part of your team, but it also says that *I'm* on it too?"

"Ah, yup," I said. "There was no way I was going to play in the games without you, *plus* you're the school president so that's gotta count for something, right? You're team captain."

Zoe shook her head. "No, that's *exactly* why I *can't* be on your team or anyone else's. I'm the president, so I can't participate. It doesn't matter if I could anyway, I really don't have the time since I'm trying to plan the Buchanan Bash in two weeks."

"Whaaaaaat?" I said. "That's a bummer. So what's that mean?"

"Nothing, except that I'm not on your team."

"Fine," I said. "Whatever then. I guess *I'll* be the team captain."

"Cool cool cool," Zoe said as she skimmed more of the form. "So it looks like your club is going to be… The Moose? What's that? Some secret term for ninjas?"

"No. Going public with a ninja clan is Wyatt's thing. I'd like to keep mine secret, especially since it's so tiny now."

"So what's The Moose?"

"Did you read it?" I asked, pointing at the form in her hands.

"Just explain it to me since you're standing right here," Zoe said.

The line for breakfast was getting longer. I could feel my breakfast sandwich slipping away from me.

Zoe's forehead wrinkled as she waited for me to explain. "Are you going to sit around in a room, cutting pictures of moose out of magazines so you could clip them to the wall? Is this a strange hobby that your parents should know about?"

"Nooo," I whined. "The Moose is just the name, but I chose that because I'd like to start a club that represents what Buchanan School is all about."

"And what's that?" Zoe asked.

"The students," I replied. "It'll be a club where *nothing* is required – no try outs or competitions. Just… *students*."

"Okaaaaaay," Zoe said, putting extra emphasis at the end of the word. "But what'll you guys do?"

"Hang out," I said. "The way I see it, kids are at their best when they're allowed to just hang out, right? Like, before school in the hallways, or in the locker room before gym. Or even sometimes during gym class when we can just walk the track and talk. So the club I want to start is a place where kids can just come… and hang out."

"Hmmm," Zoe hummed, which was a good sign because it meant that she didn't think my idea was completely coconuts.

"I realized that people become friends because they're forced to hang out in different situations," I continued. "Brayden is my best friend, but if we weren't in a bunch of the same classes together, we probably wouldn't have said a word to each other. I want to recreate that with my club. I want kids to come, and just chill."

"But who's going to join a club that doesn't do anything? How are you going to get members?"

I smiled. "By spending the budget on a candy bar. Like, it'll be set up like a salad bar, but instead of lettuce and carrots, it'll have different kinds of candy. Kids will only be allowed to take as much as a small Dixie Cup can fit. I thought it'd be cool if the group only met on Tuesdays and Thursdays too. That way nobody's binging on sweets."

Zoe paused, furrowing her brow. I think she was trying to find an argument, but couldn't. "That's... wow, that's actually not a *terrible* idea."

"I know, right?" I said joyfully. "I'm full of *not terrible* ideas."

My cousin waved the registration form at me as she turned around. "Awesome," she said. "I'll give this to Principal Davis and let him know your team is in."

Throwing a thumbs-up into the air, I flipped around ready to get in line for my breakfast sandwich, but of course the line was about three times longer than when I first got to school.

Rolling my eyes, I walked past the kitchen doors, making my way to my locker. Without eating breakfast, my stomach would probably grumble and complain all morning about it.

Wonderful.

Tuesday. 7:40 AM. My locker.

The first bell went off just as I got to my locker. After spinning the combination into the padlock, I yanked on the handle while pressing my shoulder into the door. It was my usual routine whenever I visited my locker so none of my stuff would fall out.

Sure, we have a locker clean out every two weeks, but you know how life can get busy sometimes, right? That and I was pretty sure I was feeding a small family of rodents living at the bottom of it. I'm not sure I could live with myself if I did anything to take food off their table.

Squeezing my fingers into the cold, dark, and somehow damp locker, I managed to scrape the top of my math book just enough so that it would tip into my hand.

"Gotcha!" I exclaimed as I slid the book out slowly. After it was free from the locker, I slammed the door shut with my knee since that was the spot where it clicked shut.

Suddenly, like she materialized out of thin air, Naomi was standing on the other side of my locker door.

"*Whaaaaaaa!*" I screamed, but slapped my hand over my mouth to keep from making any more of a scene.

"Nice," Naomi said. She was leaning her shoulder against the wall of lockers. "So what's up?"

I stared at her for a moment. Did she just ask me what was

up as if nothing was wrong between the two of us? As if she never ended our friendship by betraying my trust? As if she didn't crush my social life under the weight of her fist?

Naomi smiled softly at me. "Look, I know what you're thinking..."

"Do you?" I finally managed to say.

"I wasn't sure whether I should talk to you after what happened last week," Naomi said. "But then I was like, whatever, right? I know you hate me for what happened, and I don't blame you for it, but I want you to know *I'm* not mad at you anymore."

"*You're* not mad at *me?*" I asked, shocked. "What about *me?*"

Naomi laughed. "That's why I'm here," she said. "I wanted to say that I'm sorry."

I felt my heart beating faster. What was Naomi thinking? That she could just show up to my locker and say sorry and that everything would be fine between us?

I remained silent because honestly, I didn't know what to say. You want to know the truth? Naomi was such a good friend before I found out she was a Scavenger that part of me *wanted* to forgive and forget. Part of me *wanted* things to go back to normal between the two of us.

"I've been ordered to give you one last chance to join us," she said calmly. "If you do then you'll be forgiven for everything you've done."

That one made me angry. "I've done nothing!" I whispered harshly. "All *I* did was respond to all the garbage you put me through last week! I'll probably be dealing with it for the rest of my life! You and your Scavengers put a black mark on my soul that'll easily remain there for a really long time!"

Naomi pushed her lips to the side, annoyed.

But then I realized Naomi had just said she'd been *ordered* by someone else. "Wait a sec, I thought you were the *leader* of the Scavengers. Who's giving you orders?"

My ex-bestie nodded her head. "I'm the leader of the sixth grade Scavengers, but there are also seventh and eighth grade Scavengers that I have to answer to. I'm not too sure yet, but I think there are Scavengers even in high school."

"Great," I sighed. "This whole thing is going to follow me around for the rest of my life."

"Chase," Naomi said with an innocent look upon her face. "Please join us. *Please*. I know this sounds so lame, but I've missed joking around with you since last week."

Naomi had no idea how hard that statement hit me. I was doing my best to keep my face as emotionless as a chicken.

Pushing herself off the wall, Naomi said one last thing before leaving. "Also, if you don't join us, I'm not sure what *Victor's* gonna do to you."

"What?" I said as she walked away. "Wait, who's Victor? *Who's Victor?*"

Naomi turned the corner and disappeared. The bell rang a second time, signaling the start of school, which meant I was totally late for homeroom.

Tuesday. 12:15 PM. The lobby.

A few hours later, I was back in the lobby of Buchanan, waiting for the rest of my team on the steps in the nook. Each team was supposed to meet right after lunch and wait at the location of the next games. To keep everything fair, nobody knew what game was going to be played that day.

Many students were wearing their oversized masks as they gathered in the lobby. For a second time, I questioned reality.

Faith found me first and stood next to me. She was clutching her book bag straps, smiling at all the students that walked by.

"Hey," I said.

She nodded, but didn't say anything. She wasn't mad, at least not that I knew of, so I wasn't sure why she kept quiet.

I leaned my head over so that I was in her line of vision. "Hey," I repeated.

Again, she just smiled. It wasn't a fake smile, like the kind where you just tighten your mouth on both sides and nod. It was a soft smile. Real.

But it was still making me nervous. "*Why aren't you saying anything?*" I finally spit out.

Faith leaned away from me, staring at me like I was crazy. "Why do I need to say anything?" she asked.

"Because not talking is weird!" I replied.

"Why can't we sit quietly with each other?" she asked. "Why does there always need to be conversation when we're together?"

I wasn't sure I understood, and she could tell.

She went on. "You ever just sit with someone? You ever feel comfortable enough with someone that there doesn't need to be any small talk about the weather or TV shows?"

I thought for a second. "My family, I guess."

"Best friends are the same," she said to me in a way that made me feel stupid for not already getting it. "Best friends are the ones who can just hang out and be real without having to say a word."

I tried to hide my smile, but what she said made me blush a little.

She definitely noticed, but kept quiet about it.

Together and in silence, we watched as the oversized heads of kids stumbled and fumbled in the lobby, occasionally bumping into each other.

Every few seconds, a muffled, "Excuse me," or "Sorry 'bout that," would filter through their masks. It was eerie.

When Gavin and Brayden showed up, Faith and I jumped from our spot on the steps and huddled together for a quick team meeting.

"Guys, these heads are freakin' me out," I said. "I'm not sure I like the theme for today."

"I know, it's weird," Brayden said, except his voice was muffled since he was *also* wearing his large mask. "But good call on the whole 'sleeping in my mask' idea. I zonked out a few different times today and nobody suspected a thing!"

I looked at the giant kitten face on Brayden's mask, unsure where to look since I couldn't see where his eyes were. "Dude, half our classes were together this morning! Is that why you barely said anything when I talked to you?"

The giant kitten mask slowly nodded up and down like a bobble head.

Using my knuckles, I lightly backhanded Brayden's mask, enough to make him lose his balance, but not enough to actually hurt him. His dampened laugh came through wherever his air holes

48

were.

"Ew!" Faith said, looking over her shoulder. "Look at the mask *that* kid is wearing!"

My head popped up like I was a meerkat that saw an owl move in the distance. Across the lobby was some kid who had a mask with Wyatt's face on it. The eyes were eerie because each eye was looking in opposite directions.

"Who is that?" Gavin asked, but before anyone could answer, the kid removed his oversized head.

It was Wyatt. Wyatt was wearing a giant mask of his own face.

Faith giggled, putting her fist up to her mouth. "Talk about having a big head."

"Who does that?" I said. "Who wears a mask of their own face?"

"Don't you read his blog?" Gavin said. "He's been working on that thing for weeks."

I groaned. "That's definitely one corner of the Internet I'd like to forget."

At the side of the lobby, where we were standing, was a nook that was about the size of a three-car garage. There were three steps that went up and then three steps that went down on the other side. It was a place that a lot of students would hang out in before school, after lunch, or during any kind of study time in the library.

A small sound system had been hooked up so that the principal could talk into a microphone rather than shouting whatever he needed to say.

Principal Davis climbed to the top step and blew a whistle to get everyone in the lobby to pay attention.

During my entire time at Buchanan School, I had never seen the front lobby so packed with students. The entire sixth grade class had no problem filling out the gymnasium during an assembly, so you can imagine how shoulder-to-shoulder we all were in a space half that size.

As soon as everyone was mostly silent, Principal Davis tapped on the mic, making a *"thoomph, thoomph, thoomph"* sound. "Everyone, please, quiet down so we can get started. I'd like to welcome you all into this very small lobby. I guess we thought there'd be a little more room than there is, but no matter because we'll all spread out down the hallways in only a few minutes."

Zoe was standing behind the principal, gesturing for another student to join her on the steps. From the crowd, I saw a well-dressed boy hop onto the top step of the nook, next to Principal Davis and my cousin. It was Sebastian, the ex-president of Buchanan School.

"What's he doing?" I asked aloud and to nobody in particular.

Faith must've heard me because she answered. "Zoe told me she was going to give Sebastian a second chance 'cause he asked for it. She thought it would be cruel if she didn't at least *try* and throw him a bone."

"But he scammed the school," I said.

Faith nodded. "I know, but she said he came to her super bummed out. She felt sorry for him. She said she'd never seen

50

anyone so beaten and defeated."

"Well," I sighed watching Sebastian take the place by my cousin's side. "I guess that's what makes Zoe so... *Zoe*."

"Yeah," Faith agreed. "She even thinks that this could be a new Sebastian we start seeing."

"Huh," I grunted, watching the ex-president of the school stand next to the new president of the school.

"What?" Faith asked me.

"I don't know," I said, thinking about my ninja clan. "Zoe is such a natural leader. I wish that was something in my family's blood, that way maybe I could be a good leader too."

"You're kidding, right?" Faith asked. "You've been one of the best leaders I've ever seen."

Poor Faith. If only she knew that my entire ninja clan had left to the join the Scavengers. "I think you'd be surprised at how terrible of a leader I really am. You know how they say you can't teach an old dog new tricks? Well, I couldn't teach a *new* dog new tricks."

Faith folded her arms and spoke sternly but softly, probably so I wouldn't feel embarrassed. "You're confusing two different ideas. Being a good *leader* doesn't always mean being a good *teacher*."

I stared at Faith, trying not to look too dumb because I wasn't exactly sure what she meant. "Yup," I said finally.

She lightly punched my shoulder. "I can tell when your brain has a fart in it so let me explain that a little—" she said, but stopped midsentence because everyone in the lobby cheered again, staring right at the two of us.

Gavin and Brayden were standing on the step under Zoe, waiting for Faith and me to join them.

Zoe raised the microphone back to her mouth. "Anytime now, guys."

Faith and I were so into our conversation that we didn't even notice Sebastian give the microphone back to Zoe, who had obviously introduced the teams participating in the games because there were several other groups of students lined up on the steps too.

As we joined Gavin and Brayden, I looked down the line to see who it was we were going to compete against.

Wyatt was with his team, which was made up of other students I knew to be red ninjas. I could tell because all the red ninjas in the school wore red bracelets, which kind of looked like lame-o friendship bracelets.

Next down the line was Carlyle, Wyatt's cousin. He was almost the same flavor of evil that Wyatt was, except he had an obsession with being a pirate. He was the only kid in school who talked like a pirate when it *wasn't* "talk like a pirate day." The rest of his team was wearing costumes and eye patches too. I recognized most of them except for the shortest student. I couldn't see much of her face since it was hidden under an oversized bandana on her head.

A girl named Sophia was on the second to the last team. She was a hipster and so were her teammates, which was weird because hipsters are known to hate things that are popular simply because those things have become popular. I would've figured that the Spirit Week games would've been too mainstream for them, but it was possible they wanted to start some hipster club so they could sit around in a circle playing acoustic guitars and banging on drums while saying everything was "so last week."

And finally, on the last team was Jake along with his wolf pack. To put it shortly, it was a team made up of bullies that called themselves the wolf pack, and even went as far as to howl like wild animals when walking the halls.

Part of me was surprised Naomi didn't have a team.

At the foot of the steps were five grocery carts, the old school kind that looked like a metal dog cage. Each cart had a helmet hanging from the handlebar.

"Players, put your helmets on," Zoe said into the microphone. "As they're getting ready, the other two members of your teams can go ahead and take their places down the hall."

I grabbed the helmet from the grocery cart in front of me as Faith and Brayden sped off down the hall for some part of the game that I missed the explanation for.

"What are those guys gonna do?" I asked.

Gavin snatched the helmet from me. "Where's your head at, dude? Didn't ya hear Zoe tell the rules?"

"Totes, man," I said, squeezing my hands around the handlebar of the grocery cart. "But I wanna hear you repeat them so I know *you* know the rules."

Gavin pressed air through his lips, making a "*pfffff*" sound because he knew I was lying. "Whatever, man. You and I are the ones competing in this race. One of us rides and one of us pushes to the first checkpoint challenge."

"Cool," I said. "What's at the first checkpoint?"

"Brayden will be waiting with a bucket of baked beans and an apple."

"Awesome. Wait... why?"

Gavin took a deep breath as he clipped the bottom of his helmet. "We'll have to bob for the apple in the bucket of baked beans."

I leaned my head over and stuck out my bottom lip. "Pretty nasty, but alright," I said, trying to keep a positive attitude. "What's after that?"

"We switch places in the grocery cart," Gavin said, hopping into the metal cage of the cart. "Then we race to the second checkpoint, where Faith will be waiting with a balloon and shaving cream."

"Because we need to shave the balloon," I said, guessing the second checkpoint challenge.

Gavin glanced over his shoulder as he grabbed the front of the grocery cart. "Bingo, partner," he said.

"What do these games have to do with Spirit Week?" I asked, revving the grocery cart handlebar like it was a motorcycle. The other teams were already set up next to us and ready to go.

"Nothing," Gavin said. "It's all just a bunch of random stuff to make us all look like fools!"

I nodded.

Zoe raised an air horn over her head and paused. Everyone fell silent because they thought she was going to say something, but she never did, pushing the button instead.

HOOOOOOOOOOOONK!

Tuesday. 12:23 PM. The race.

My body jumped forward after Zoe honked the air horn, flinching the way it does at the start of any race. Then with all the power I could muster, I shoved the grocery cart forward.

The other sixth graders were pressed against the walls as they hooted and hollered.

All five teams were side by side, banging our carts into each other like we were driving bumper cars.

"Watch it, Chase!" Gavin shouted as he ducked his head lower. "You're gonna get m'fingers pinched!"

Sophia pulled ahead of everyone, thrusting her cart down the first hallway as students cheered her on from the sidelines.

I stole a peek over my shoulder to see where Wyatt's cart was. I was happy to see that he was bringing up the rear, completely in last place. Hopefully his team would just get eliminated first – that way I wouldn't have to worry about him creating a public ninja club for his clan at all.

Jake's cart smashed into the side of mine, and I'm pretty sure it was on purpose because he did it again immediately.

I didn't want to risk tipping my grocery cart over so I ran faster to try and get ahead of Jake, but his passenger grabbed the side of my cart.

"Hey!" I shouted. "Let go! You can't do that!"

The kid in Jake's cart laughed as he jerked our cart back and forth, making it wobble like crazy.

Gavin grabbed the boy's fingers, peeling them away from our cart. As soon as he lost his grip, Gavin raised his leg over the side of the metal grate and pushed Jake's cart away.

Sparks flew as Jake's grocery cart scraped against the metal lockers. He fell behind just enough that I didn't have to worry about a second attack.

I'm pretty sure Principal Davis was going to regret giving this race the go-ahead after seeing what kind of damage it caused.

"Easy now!" Gavin shouted, pointing at the end of the hallway. "Slow down! You're gonna take the turn too fast!"

Digging my feet into the carpet, I tried slowing down, but my shoes weren't getting any traction. They slid across the floor like I was skating on ice.

"Dag gummit!" Gavin shouted, dropping to the bottom of the cart in a fetal position.

Our grocery cart crashed into the brick wall at the end of the hallway. My body flew forward, but the grocery cart stopped it with its handlebar.

Students in the hall turned their heads away instantly, groaning in pain for Gavin and me.

"C'mon," Gavin said, sitting back on his knees. "Jake's gainin' on us!"

"But," I said, clutching at my stomach. "My organs! *All* of my organs!"

Jake turned the corner with ease, steering his cart like it was nothing. As he ran by, he laughed.

Pulling the cart away from the wall, I shoved it forward again, doing my best to gain speed with long strides.

"Okay," Gavin said. "I see Brayden and the bucket of baked beans just up ahead. Start slowin' down now!"

This time I took Gavin's advice and instead of trying to skid to a stop, I slowed myself down to a jog and then to a speed walk until we finally came to a complete stop.

Brayden helped Gavin out of the cart. "Ok, get the apple! Sophia's over by her bucket still trying to grab it! You guys can pull ahead right now!"

Gavin looked at me. "Go ahead, you got this!"

I stared at the bucket of cold baked beans, horrified. A thick bubble formed at the center of the slop, and then popped, splashing some of the cold baked bean juice on my clothes. "Sick, man! That thing just burped! I'm not putting my face in that! *You* do it!"

"Absolutely not," Gavin said, upset. "Ain't no way I'm snatchin' an apple from there."

"*One* of you has to do it!" Brayden said frantically. "If you don't, then we'll lose the race for sure!"

Gavin tightened his lips and looked me in the eye. Holding his fist in the air, he spoke. "Best outta three?"

Kids cheered in the hallway. Sophia was standing by the side of her slop bucket, her hair and face dripping with baked beans as she held an apple between her teeth. The only clean parts of her face were the whites of her eyes as she blinked. She looked like a monster.

"Fine!" I said, punching my open palm with my other fist.

"Rock, paper, scissors!" Gavin and I said at the same time.

Gavin threw rock while I threw scissors.

"No!" I shouted.

I heard Jake's voice laugh loudly from behind me, which meant his teammate had clenched the apple from the bucket of beans.

Again, Gavin and I slammed our fists into our palms. "Rock, paper, scissors!"

Gavin threw rock again. I threw paper.

"Ha!" I shouted, slapping Gavin's rock with my open hand.

For a third time, Gavin and I chanted together. "Rock, paper, scissors!"

"Booyah ha!" I said, victorious because I had thrown scissors against Gavin throwing paper.

Gavin grunted, but didn't waste any time. He clutched the sides of the bucket and splashed his face into the baked beans, making a nasty "*splorch*" sound.

I looked back down the hall we had come from, trying to see where Wyatt was, but he was so far behind that he hadn't even turned the corner yet.

Gavin pulled his face from the beans, took a deep breath, and plunged back into the glorious mess of syrupy goodness. I'm not gonna lie – it was pretty funny to watch.

Finally, Gavin stood up straight, holding an apple in his mouth. Round beans fell back into the bucket as he wiped them from his eyes.

"Go!" Brayden shouted. "You can wipe them off when you're done!"

I jumped into the metal cage of the grocery cart since it was Gavin's turn to push.

Shaking his head like a dog, Gavin managed to get enough of the baked beans off his face to see clearly. Then he grabbed the handlebars of the grocery cart and thrust forward so hard that I fell against the back of the cart.

The ceiling tiles flew by as I watched them from the bottom of the cart.

It was actually kind of pleasant.

Tuesday. 12:27 PM. The second checkpoint.

After the second turn, I saw Faith standing at the end of the hallway next to a desk that had three balloons floating above it.

"There!" I said.

Gavin turned the cart sideways and slid it to a stop like a car in an action movie. It was almost like he had done it before.

After fumbling out of the cart, I stepped up to the desk with the floating balloons. Each balloon had shaving cream smeared on it. "Okay," I said to Faith. "What do I do?"

Faith handed me a plastic scraper. "Use this as a razor and shave the balloon without popping it. You get three shots."

"What happens if I pop all three?" I asked, taking the scraper from Faith.

"Then our team just gets a ten second penalty in the race," Faith explained. "So once you guys cross the finish line, you'll have to wait ten seconds before it counts. Anyone that finishes within those ten seconds comes in before you."

"Got it," I said, lowering my body into more of a horse stance. Holding the scraper in my right hand, I took the balloon with my left and turned it slightly.

"Are you sure you got it?" Faith said, cocking an eyebrow.

"Of course!" I replied. "I've seen my dad do this a million times. How hard could it be?" I said confidently as slid the plastic scraper down the side of the balloon's face.

The sound of rubber getting stretched came from beneath my scraper as little balls of sweat formed on my forehead. My hand holding the balloon started shaking as my other hand cramped up around the scraper. I guess I was more nervous than I thought. I could be wrong, but it felt like shaving a balloon was just as hard as disarming a bomb.

Jake had already left the balloon checkpoint. I had no doubt that his team was going to come in first place.

Sophia was nearly finished shaving her balloon as her hipster friends cheered her on from the sidelines.

Carlyle and his pirate team were just catching up to us.

Wyatt was still nowhere to be seen, which didn't actually make me feel better. The entire race had been so distracting that it was possible he passed Gavin and me without us noticing.

Ever so carefully, I wiped the scraper off on the edge of the desk, and went in again. There was only one strip I had cleaned off, but nearly thirty seconds had already passed.

"*Careful*," I whispered, touching the scraper to the balloon. "*Caaaaaareful…*"

And then it happened. The balloon exploded.
POP!

Shaving cream splattered across the entire front of my body and my life flashed before my eyes. It wasn't very long, but still kind of depressing.

Everyone laughed, covering their faces and flinching for me.

I stood there shocked as shaving cream soaked into my clothes and hair.

He was trying to hide it, but I could hear Gavin snickering behind me.

"C'mon, dude!" Faith said, slapping my shoulder and bringing my head out of the clouds. "Round two! Go!"

I stared at the other balloons with shaving cream on them, already feeling stressed and shaky at the thought of doing it again. So instead, I took the scraper in my hand and jabbed at the other two balloons, popping them.

Faith squealed a laugh as she covered her face with her arms.

Gavin pushed the grocery cart back up to me. "That's one way of doing it!" he said. "Now get in! Carlyle's the only one behind us!"

I jumped in, scanning the hall ahead of us. Jake was already gone, probably at the finish line. Sophia's grocery cart was turning the last corner. Wyatt's cart was still out of the picture. And Carlyle was quickly scraping his balloon clean.

There was a short path ahead of us where the hallway squeezed tighter. There weren't any students watching in that spot because it was just wide enough to get our grocery carts through and nothing else.

I clutched the cage at the front of the grocery cart as Gavin plowed forward into the narrow passage. There wasn't any time to wipe myself clean from the shaving cream, and Gavin was still dripping with baked bean juice. It was the most random, disgusting adventure I had ever been apart of, and I was loving every second of it.

Until Gavin caught his shoulder in the super narrow hallway.

Falling forward, Gavin turned the grocery cart and pushed the handlebar one last time, launching me at a hundred miles per hour down the final stretch of the race.

The cart shook uncontrollably underneath me as I did my best to steer the steel death trap from inside by leaning left and right.

Like a mighty Spartan warrior, I screamed. At least, that's how I wanted to sound. Pretty sure I sounded like a frightened three-year-old.

Students dove aside as my cart barreled past them.

"Gangway!" I shouted, trying to come up with a plan to stop the cart once I crossed the finish line. "Get outta the way!"

I was so close I could taste the victory, or at least the only victory my team could achieve at that point, which would be *not* coming in dead last. It tasted a lot like shaving cream.

There was only about fifty feet between my cart and where Zoe was standing waving a black and white checkered flag.

Jake was standing with the rest of his team behind my cousin. Sophia was also there, wiping her face clean of the baked bean slop.

And there, with a goofy grin on his face, was Wyatt and the rest of his team. I was right – he must've gotten ahead of Gavin and me when we were distracted by the checkpoint challenges.

It was only down to Carlyle and me, and I could hear him shouting.

"Yar, matey!" Carlyle growled.

Ugh! He was talking like a pirate again. I *hated* when anyone talked like a pirate. There's something about it that makes me think of nails scratching a chalkboard.

He was only about fifteen feet behind me, waving a pirate flag as he rode in the metal cage of his grocery cart. The shorter student from his team that I didn't recognize was furiously sprinting down the hall, pushing the cart.

"Outta the way, ya land lubber!" Carlyle shouted over the sound of metal grocery carts clashing. "This victory be in the palm of me fist! Ye already lost, Mister Cooper!"

The finish line was coming up fast as I sailed forward in my unpiloted cart. Carlyle was still half a hallway behind me. It was still possible for me to beat the pirate poser! All I had to do was keep my grocery cart from falling over.

Which is exactly what happened next.

I'm not sure what it was, but my cart caught something hard

61

in the carpet. You ever hit a rock with a skateboard? The entire world stops moving for that split second as you fly through the air, waiting to scrape your palms on the ground.

Like a ragdoll, I tumbled out of my grocery cart, fumbling to a complete stop right in front of the finish line. Carlyle's cart rolled past, securing their place in the rest of the games.

Painfully reaching forward, I crawled over the finish line dead last. That was it. My team was done, and we were going to be eliminated with no chance at keeping Wyatt from winning the Spirit Week grand prize.

I could tell by the expression on Zoe's face that she was disappointed when she helped me off the ground.

Sebastian was already on the microphone announcing the winners of the race. Apparently Wyatt's team had come in first place.

As I wrung out the shaving cream at the bottom of my hoodie, Wyatt came up to gloat, already wearing the first place bright green ribbon. He was in the middle of slurping a spoonful of cereal that he got from who knows where? From the smell, I could tell it was Cookie Dough Delight.

For the record, I *hate* Cookie Dough Delight. It was like crispy rice cereal with little balls of dried out cookie dough. Trust me – it wasn't as awesomesauce as it sounded.

"Nice effort," Wyatt said. "I would give that performance a D minus. Not *quite* an F, but not far from it."

"How'd you come in first?" I said, feeling the weight of utter defeat press down on my shoulders.

"I raced a good race," Wyatt replied, shoveling another spoonful of dried cookie dough balls into his mouth. "You and Gavin must've been sidetracked somewhere along the race."

The rock, paper, scissors games must've been where Wyatt took the lead. Gavin and I were so wrapped up at that point that a car could've crashed into the building and we wouldn't have noticed.

"And we crossed the finish line *way* before anyone else did," Wyatt said. He waved his hand at someone nearby to get their attention. "Was that awesome? I mean, we did our best and totes came in first, but I'm pretty sure we could've done better."

Gross. Wyatt was practicing what's called the "humble

brag." It's when someone brags about how amazing they are by putting it in the form of self criticism.

"All's well that ends well though," Wyatt sneered.

"That saying only counts if the end result is a good one," I said.

"But it is!" Wyatt said. "At least for me and my team!"

Suddenly, everyone in the lobby gasped at the same time. Wyatt spun so fast to see what the fuss was about that some of the milk from his cereal spilled onto the floor.

Principal Davis raised his hands into the air to try and calm everyone down. "Students, please!" he said sternly. "Please back away and give us some room."

Standing on my tippy toes, I tried to see over everyone, but there were too many people in front of me.

"Please!" Principal Davis said again. "Calm down and take two steps back!"

The students in the lobby did as he ordered and pushed backward.

After squeezing myself past a few of the taller kids, I could finally see what everyone had been shocked by.

Carlyle was standing with his arms folded behind Principal Davis. One of the students on his team was on the other side of the principal. It was the shorter kid from earlier that I didn't recognize and now I understood why.

It was because it *wasn't* a student! It was the Korean *janitor!*

I was close enough to hear Principal Davis scolding the old woman. "Miss Chen-Jung," he said. "You're retiring this year, and *this* is the legacy you want to leave behind?"

Miss Chen-Jung scrunched her face, making it look like a black hole appeared at the center of her head. "Pirates forever, yo!"

Carlyle stood silently on the other side of the principal.

"You know what this means, right?" Principal Davis asked Carlyle.

"That Miss Chen-Jung is gonna get fired?" Carlyle asked.

Principal Davis laughed. "No," he said. "Miss Chen-Jung is going to be fine. She shouldn't have played in the games with you, but there's no way I'm going to discipline a sixty-five year old woman for a silly act like that. You and your team, on the other hand, will be disqualified from the rest of the Spirit Week games."

Zoe stepped forward with a glint in her eye. "Which means Chase and his team are still in!"

Principal Davis nodded.

I heard Wyatt crunch down on his spoon. Without looking at me, he spoke. "You're lucky, but luck won't help you next time."

Faith came out of nowhere and nearly tackled me to the floor with a hug. "You did it! You failed miserably, but still managed to not *entirely* lose!"

"Yaaay," I sang sarcastically as I twirled my finger in the air.

Gavin joined us, cleaning his face off with a towel. Brayden was behind him, walking with Dani, the student council secretary.

"Man, that was a close one," Brayden said.

"At least you're not out," Dani crooned with a smile, staring at Brayden.

"I just can't believe Wyatt got first place," Gavin said. "You guys think he cheated somehow?"

Dani looked at Gavin. "Oh no," she said. "I watched him turn that last corner *where Gavin fell*. Wyatt ran across the finish line fair and square. Everyone else saw him do it too."

Gavin pouted, embarrassed.

I took a deep breath and watched Wyatt celebrate with the other members of his team. I couldn't believe we had come in last place because it's not like we didn't try. Carlyle had an old lady on his team, and they *still* managed to beat us fair and square.

This whole thing was going to be tougher than I thought.

Tuesday. 12:45 PM. The cafeteria.

Brayden and I were in the middle of a conversation when we stepped into the cafeteria, which was bustling with activity. Since the grocery cart race ended a few minutes early, the sixth graders were told to "hang loose" in the cafeteria. At least that's what Principal Davis called it. I think he meant "hang out" or something.

"I'm not saying they shouldn't be allowed to wear them," Brayden said, "But I stand behind the idea that if you're gonna wear the uniform, you *gotta* sell the cookies."

I shook my head. "Your brother's a *weird* dude."

"You have no idea," Brayden said.

We stopped right inside the cafeteria doors. Melvin, Gidget, and Slug were sitting at a table at the far end of the other room.

I sighed. "I can't believe the ninja clan is down to a handful of kids."

"Why not?" Brayden asked. "Actually, I think it's better this way."

"Wouldn't it be better if it were the size of the red ninja clan?"

"They got like, a hundred kids in that ninja clan," Brayden said. "It won't be long before it comes crashing in on itself. At some point, someone will think they can do a better job of running it than Wyatt, and once that happens, the whole thing will crumble."

I shook my head. "I dunno, man. Wyatt seems to be keeping them together pretty well," I said, feeling sorry for myself. "He might just be a better leader than I am."

Brayden paused, and I regretted saying something that had to do with *feelings*. Finally, he spoke. "Why go big? That didn't work last time with you. What if you kept it small? Like a tightly balled fist? Less is more, right? Don't you think a smaller band of ninjas is more effective than an army of a hundred?"

I shrugged.

After weaving through the crowd, we finally sat on the bench along with the new members of my ninja clan.

Slug leaned his head against one of his hands, struggling to keep his eyes open. Gidget still had her face pointed at the screen on her phone. And Melvin was scribbling some chicken scratch in a small notebook.

"So why aren't we training in the wrestling room?" Gidget asked from behind her cellphone.

"Because being a ninja is about more than how many punches and kicks you've thrown," I said, dropping my book bag on the lunch table.

Gidget stuffed her phone into the small pocket of her book bag and hoisted the strap over her shoulder. "Later, guys. It's been a blast, and by 'a blast,' I mean it's been supes boring. I got better things to do with my time."

Great. Another ninja quit my ninja clan. It must be what all the cool kids are doing.

"What better things do you have to do?" Slug asked.

"I dunno," Gidget replied. "Deal with it."

Gidget walked to the front of the cafeteria and joined a table of other girls who were hypnotized by their cellphones. It was very possible they were all just texting each other.

"Being a twin must be hard work," Melvin said to Slug.

"Easy," Slug said, wrinkles appearing on his forehead. "Gidget might have a chip on her shoulder, but she's still my sister."

Melvin nodded. He turned back to me. "So Wyatt came in first," he stated.

"He did," I said, still unsure about the whole race. "But did you see him cross the finish line?"

I was hoping that Melvin had some kind of proof that Wyatt had bypassed the race and just appeared at the finish line, but he didn't. "Yeah. I watched him and his buddy cross the line in their grocery cart."

"I was afraid of that," I sighed.

"Tell ya what," Melvin said. "I'll ask around and see what others say about the race."

"You'd do that?" Brayden asked.

"Of course," Melvin said. "I'm a reporter. Asking questions is what I'm best at."

The rest of the time we were in the cafeteria, we were mostly quiet. After Gidget removed herself from the clan, I didn't really feel like talking about honor and strength and things like that, because honestly, I was beginning to think I didn't understand it as well I thought I did.

I mean, it was only the second day with the kids in my new ninja clan, and I'd already lost one member.

Wednesday. 7:35 AM. The cafeteria.

After getting dropped off to school by my dad, I went straight into the kitchen to grab some fries and a juice. I know what you're thinking – *fries* for breakfast? *Who does that?* And my answer is this – if the school thought it was bad for me, then they wouldn't make them in the morning. Besides, the box of OJ made it part of a balanced breakfast, right? Yeah, we'll go with that.

It was day three of Spirit Week, which I was actually super pumped about because the theme was the future, and that meant I could dress like it was the year 3,000. I had spent the night before crafting a robotic looking costume out of cardboard, aluminum foil, and flexible metal ducts that I stuck my arms into.

I looked super sick.

"Chase! Over here!" my cousin called from a lunch table a few rows away.

Shuffling my feet across the ground, I walked over to the table that my friends were sitting at. Zoe was talking rapidly, stopping every few sentences so Gavin could write down what she said.

Faith was munching on a slice of breakfast pizza. When she saw me, she formed the biggest smile I'd ever seen, showing me all the pizza sauce and chewed up cheese in her teeth on purpose. It made me honk out a laugh, which then made *her* laugh too.

Fortunately, she covered her mouth so none of the pizza would fly out of it.

And Brayden was in the middle of some huge story he was telling to Dani. I could tell because when Brayden gets into a story, he makes big gestures with his hands.

"Nice costume," Zoe said. "Those arms are going to make it difficult to do anything though."

"I know," I said, taking the seat across from Faith. "I'll probably dump the whole costume before going to homeroom. It's more trouble than it's worth. I mean, I *know* I look way super cool, but I'm not sure I'm willing to pay the price of comfort for it."

Nobody really laughed at my lame joke.

"So…" I said, stuffing my mouth with a handful of fries. "What's the game plan for today?"

Zoe chuckled. "Nice try."

"Come on," I joked. "What good is having a cousin that's president if she doesn't help me out here and there?"

Zoe made a face at me. "Is this a small preview of what we're going to be like as adults? Are you telling me that you'll be a degenerate loser constantly calling me to bail you out of jail for some type of petty crime?"

I cracked a wicked smile. "Mayhaps," I said, combining the words "maybe" and "perhaps."

"Mayhaps isn't a word," Zoe said as she read what Gavin was writing down. "Don't write 'mayhaps!' Don't give power to Chase's weird language!"

"I like the word," Gavin said honestly. "It's goin' on the notepad."

I started whining like a baby, playfully of course. "Come onnnnn, cousin! Didn't you say you owed me for slapping me in front of everyone last week?"

That actually happened.

Zoe narrowed her eyes. "I *already* apologized for that, but *you* said we were even since I only slapped you because you took credit for my pizza party. A party pizza, which BTW, cost almost a thousand bucks of my own money that I scrimped and saved for all year."

I scratched the back of my head, feeling a bit shameful. It was the Scavengers that were responsible for snagging Zoe's pizza party away from her, and since she still didn't know they existed, I didn't want to come clean about exactly what happened.

I knew if I acted sad, she'd drop the subject, even though it was *me* who brought it up. "You're right," I said, trailing off.

The first bell went off outside in the lobby, which meant school was about five minutes away from starting.

Dani jumped up from the table as if the bell had scared her. She moved so fast that her knee bumped against the bottom of the table and made her fall to the floor.

"Whoa!" Brayden said. "You okay?"

"Yup," Dani said, laughing at her own fumble. "The bell just scared me, that's all." She bounced up from the floor. "I gotta go though. I need to go to the bathroom before homeroom. I'll see you at lunch, okay?"

Brayden blushed. "Okay. Later."

I took the last little handful of fries on my tray and shoved them into my mouth, chewing loudly on purpose to annoy everyone. Too bad I didn't pick up a napkin from the kitchen because my fingers were crazy greasy. I almost wiped them off on the front of my hoodie, but then I remembered that my mom *hated* when I did that.

I leaned back, holding my box of OJ over my mouth, chugging every last bit of it.

"It isn't a race, guy," Zoe said, grossed out.

Her comment wasn't meant to be funny, but I still laughed... in the middle of a gulp, which made me cough some of the mixture of OJ and fries out of my mouth.

Zoe jumped from the table, covering her mouth and gagging.

Everyone else laughed about it though, even me.

"Great," I said. "I got juice comin' out of my nose."

My cousin had her hands on her hips, staring at the ceiling because she refused to look at my face. "Clean yourself up," she laughed. "Because that's *so* sick!"

Wiping my chin with my sleeve, I got up from the table, pulling my book bag over my shoulder at the same time. "Alright, I'll go wash the decadent orange juice infused mashed potatoes off my face," I chuckled. "I'll see you guys back here after lunch."

Wednesday. 7:43 AM. The hallways.

After leaving the lunchroom, I rushed down the hallway to find the nearest bathroom. Most of the OJ and fries got on the table so there wasn't really much for me to wash off, if anything really, but losing that last chug of juice left me thirsty. I turned the corner to grab a sip of brown water from one of the many rusty water fountains in the school.

As I got closer, I saw Dani walking down the opposite direction of the hallway, away from the restrooms.

"Hey, Dani, wait up!" I called out.

Dani stopped in the hall. She spun around and shot me a smile. "Hi," she said.

Have you ever run into anyone and then say hi because it's the polite thing to do, but then you realize you have nothing else to say? That's what happened next.

I stared at Dani, trying to think of something, *anything*, to say. "So…"

Dani leaned her head forward. "Mm-hmm? You called my name and told me to wait up."

"I know," I said in a soft murmur.

Dani never broke eye contact even though I did. I could *feel* her looking at me. "So… what? Did you want to say something to me?" she asked.

If Zoe were here, she'd whistle and then whisper, "*Awkwaaaaaaard...*"

In a panic, I thought I'd try to be funny. Pointing at the water fountain, I said, "Good. This is good water. Brown water's the best. I call it gravy water."

Dani's face went from curious to slightly concerned for her safety. "Okaaaaay..."

At that instant, the men's restroom door swung open. A small part of me was relieved because I could use the distraction as a way to escape that awkward exchange. But as if fate had it in for me, Wyatt peeked out.

Of course.

Wyatt stopped in the doorway of the restroom, carrying a rectangular manila envelope in his hand and still proudly displaying his first place ribbon pinned to his shirt. He had a paranoid and suspicious way about him, but I didn't think anything of it because when *doesn't* he look like that?

Another moment of head crushing silence passed as the

three of us looked back and forth at each other.

Wyatt pointed between Dani and me. "What's going on here? What're you guys doing?"

"What are *you* doing?" I replied. Not my best comeback, I know.

"I just went to the bathroom!" Wyatt said sternly. "That's not weird. What's weird are two students waiting for me to come out of it! *That's* weird!"

"Nasty," I said. "Nobody was waiting for you out here."

Wyatt wiped his wet hands on his shirt.

Please just be water because you washed your hands, I thought.

Wyatt stepped out and gave Dani an evil eye. "What're *you* staring at?"

Dani huffed, shaking her head like she was more offended than annoyed. Without saying another word, she turned and sped off down the hall.

"Chicks, am I right?" Wyatt said, smashing his palm against the water fountain switch. He slurped at the rusty brown water that gushed from the spigot.

"Whatever," I said, glancing at the clock on the wall. I only had about thirty seconds to make it to homeroom before getting counted tardy.

I pulled my book bag straps tighter over my shoulders and took a step.

"You know, it's not enough for me to win these games," Wyatt said.

Stopping, I looked over my shoulder at him.

"No," he went on, "I don't think victory is enough, unless the victory comes with a side of Chase Cooper's failure. Mmm, yeah. That sounds good. I'll have *that*."

I cringed. Wyatt was known to say some pretty messed up stuff, but that was easily one of the more meaner things I've heard come out of his mouth.

But I took the high road and walked away saying nothing in return.

Wednesday. 12:20 PM. The cafeteria.

After meeting up with my team, we stepped into the cafeteria and took our spots on the stage. Zoe was up front speaking into a microphone.

"Who's ready for a quiz show?" Zoe hollered into the mic as everyone in the audience cheered.

The sixth grade students of Buchanan School were all seated in metal fold out chairs that had been lined in rows. There had to be over a hundred rows of seats.

On the stage were the four remaining teams. Jake's team was at the far left. Wyatt's team was next in line. Sophia's team was right next to us. And we were the last on the stage at the far right. Each table had a microphone and a light up buzzer placed on top of it.

"At least this game is clean," Gavin said, leaning back in his metal chair. "I was pickin' baked beans outta my ears until bedtime last night!"

"*That*," Faith said pausing, "is nasty."

Zoe jumped off the stage and took a seat at a desk that was right at the front of the cafeteria, facing the teams. She popped her microphone into a tiny stand on the desk and shuffled through a stack of notecards. "Sebastian is going to come around to each team with a basket. If you have a cellphone, please place it in the basket. You'll get it back at the end of the game."

Sebastian stepped out of the shadows, carrying an empty blue milk crate.

"No way," Jake shouted. "How do I know you're not gonna mess with it?"

Zoe set down the notecards and leaned forward, speaking clearly into the microphone. "We'll leave the phones right at the front of the stage. They'll never be out of your view the entire time."

The members of each team groaned, but did as Zoe ordered. It only made sense. If this game was a quiz, anyone who had a smartphone could easily look up the answer to any question.

After Sebastian set the milk crate of phones down, my cousin continued. "Let's get started, shall we? The first team to get to seven points wins. After I ask the question, players will buzz in if they think they have the answer. Wait until I call on you to answer, or you might end up answering on accident if someone else hit their buzzer before you. Okay?"

Most of us on the stage nodded together.

"Okay," Zoe said, lifting the first notecard to her face. "President Buchanan was never married, so *who* was the first lady?"

I slammed my hand down on the buzzer, and then shouted my answer into the mic. "His niece! His niece was the first lady!"

Zoe tightened her lips. "I'm sorry, Chase, you weren't the first one to buzz in."

I looked across the stage. Wyatt's buzzer was lit up in a bright blue color.

"Wyatt's team," Zoe said reluctantly. "Do you have an answer?"

A smile creaked across Wyatt's face. He stared right at me as he leaned forward and spoke. "The first lady during President Buchanan's term… was his niece."

"Nice one," Faith said.

At the side of the stage, Sebastian was at a dry erase board keeping score. He drew a line under Wyatt's name since Wyatt's team had scored the first point.

The cafeteria full of sixth graders clapped lazily.

"Second question," Zoe said. "Male Moose are known to

shed *what* every winter?"

The buzzers buzzed.

"Jake's team," Zoe said. "What's your answer?"

"Bones!" Jake said with confidence.

"Can anything shed bones?" Brayden asked, leaning toward us.

"That'd be freaky," I said, shuddering at the thought of a blob of moose fur slithering away from the bones it had just shed.

Jake's team gave themselves a round of applause, but Zoe put a stop to that immediately.

"I'm sorry, that answer is incorrect," Zoe said as students in the lunchroom snickered.

Everyone's buzzers went off again.

"Chase's team!" Zoe said joyfully.

"Fur," I said.

"No!" Faith scolded. "Moose shed their *antlers!*"

"I mean—" I started to say, but my cousin cut me off.

"That answer is incorrect," Zoe said.

Then Wyatt's buzzer went off. "Antlers," he said calmly.

Zoe nodded at Sebastian who put another mark under Wyatt's name on the dry erase board.

Wyatt exchanged high fives with each member of his team. Some of them tried giving him the bro-fist instead, which led to that awkward moment when fists are bumping open palms.

Zoe went on. "How many dimples does a regulation golf ball have?"

The buzzers fell silent for a moment.

"How does anyone even know the answer to something like that?" I asked.

Again, Wyatt's buzzer went off. He spoke before Zoe called on him. "Three hundred and sixty six," he said with his eyes half shut and a cocky smile.

Sebastian put another mark for Wyatt's team.

"I golf during the summer with my dad," Wyatt said, holding his palms up as his teammates clenched victory fists.

"A group of crows is called a *what*?" Zoe asked.

Again, the buzzers were silent, but only for a moment because Wyatt buzzed in... *again*.

"A group of crows is called a murder!" he answered.

76

"That's not right," Gavin said, folding his arms on the table.

"That's *correct*," Zoe said.

Gavin flinched forward. "*Really?*"

"That's so dark," Faith said.

Wyatt had four marks under his name on the dry erase board. The other three teams had yet to score a single point.

Zoe flipped out another notecard. "How many trips did the Titanic take before sinking?"

"Is that a trick question?" I asked Faith as she pressed the buzzer.

"Zero!" Faith said, but covered her mouth instantly.

Wyatt's buzzer was already lit up. "Zero," he said.

Zoe's face was clearly frustrated. "Correct!" she said, pretending to be excited.

Another mark went under Wyatt's name on the scoreboard.

Zoe didn't hesitate with the next question. "Who sculpted Mount Rushmore?"

Wyatt's buzzer went off almost before Zoe was even finished asking her question.

Everyone in the room looked at Wyatt, waiting for him to speak.

"Aren't you going to call on me?" Wyatt asked Zoe sarcastically. "We can only answer if you call on us."

Zoe squeezed the bridge of her nose. "Wyatt's team, what's your answer?"

"Gutzon de la Mothe Borglum," he said, slowly and with an accent.

Zoe paused. "That's right."

"There's no way he's *not* cheating," Brayden said. "He's getting his answers from somewhere, it's so obvi. He used that Mount Rushmore dude's *whole* name! Gustaf du la Mothman, or whatever!"

"But everyone had to give up their cellphones," I said.

"Then someone must be feeding him the answers," Brayden said. "Whoever's helping him should get thrown in detention for the rest of the year."

The scoreboard had six marks under Wyatt's name. With only seven points needed to win, his team was one away from victory.

I hovered my hand over the buzzer, ready to push it down before Zoe even finished her next question.

Zoe flipped up another card. "How many bones in the human skull?"

Finally, our buzzer went off.

"Chase's team," Zoe said.

"Twenty two!" I said, grabbing the base of the microphone, hoping I was right because I wasn't sure why I chose that number.

"Correct!" Zoe said, doing her best to conceal her excitement.

Sebastian put a mark under my name on the scoreboard.

"Don't ask me how I knew that," I said to my team.

"What does a meteorologist study?" Zoe asked.

Again, I slammed my buzzer before she finished speaking.

"Meteors!" I said after Zoe called on my team.

Zoe gasped, and I knew I had gotten the answer wrong.

Wyatt's buzzer went off again. He looked at me as if he felt sorry for me while he answered the question. "I'm afraid a meteorologist studies the *weather*, Chase."

"Correct," Zoe said, tapping her notecards on her desk.

"Groaaaan," Faith sighed.

"It's fine," I said, trying to remain positive. "We just have to *not* lose in order to stay in the games. We've got one point already – only six more to go." I raised my fists and pretended to cheer. "Yay, math!"

Zoe continued. "Wyatt's team wins, but there are still three teams remaining, which brings us to sudden elimination."

"Sudden what?" I repeated.

"Sudden elimination," Gavin said. "It means—"

"I *know* what it means!" I said, upset. "First wrong answer loses!"

"Not exactly," Zoe said. The mic at my table must've picked up my voice. "In this version, the last team out is the loser. I'll ask the question. One team will answer. If they get it right, they advance to tomorrow's game. If they get it wrong, they won't be eliminated. They'll just remain in the quiz for the next question."

I sat forward, hovering my hand over the buzzer again. Jake and Sophia did the same thing over their own buzzers. Wyatt and his team left the stage through the side doors.

78

Zoe paused, taking a breath. "What year did World War II end?"

Our hands all slammed on the buzzers, but it was Jake who hit it first.

"1492!" he shouted.

"Wow," Faith said. "That's so wrong that I'm embarrassed *for* him."

"Incorrect!" Zoe said, and then immediately asked the next question. "What's the largest country in the world?"

Hands slapped buzzers across the stage. Jake got to it first again.

"Texas!" he said.

"No!" Zoe said, pointing her finger at Jake's team.

Gavin stood from our table so quickly that his chair slid backward. "*Texas is a state, not a country! What's the matter with you?*"

Zoe flipped another card. "Name one bird that can't fly!"

Hands slammed on the table, but Sophia answered before Zoe called on her team. "Penguins!"

I looked at Jake's buzzer, which wasn't lit up. Neither was mine. That meant it actually *was* Sophia's turn to answer.

"Correct!" Zoe shouted, getting excited. "Gratz to your team, Sophia. You've secured a spot in tomorrow's game."

Sophia's team celebrated with hugs as they left through the same door that Wyatt's team did.

Only two teams remained on stage – Jake's team, and mine.

"What's the main ingredient in glass?" Zoe asked.

I slammed on the buzzer, but Jake beat me to it again.

"No!" I snipped.

"*Glass!*" Jake answered, fully realizing he meant to say something else. "I mean—"

"Incorrect!" Zoe said, shaking her head while holding back a laugh.

"Glass is the main ingredient in glass, huh?" Faith hollered.

Zoe jumped in with the next question. "What's the closest star to Earth?"

The buzzers were silent for a second. I think Jake and I were confused by the question.

Everyone in the cafeteria stared at the stage, waiting for one of us to answer.

"One of you might as well press the buzzer," Zoe said.

Faith pushed my hand down on the buzzer.

"Chase's team," Zoe said. "What's your answer?"

I looked at Jake, whose eyes looked like they were shooting lasers at me.

"Well?" Gavin whispered. "Just answer. If ya get it wrong, Zoe'll just ask another question."

"But I don't want to get it wrong!" I said.

"Then what's the hold up?" Faith asked. "The answer is Proxima Centauri!"

"First," I said, "That's amazing that you know that much about stars."

Faith blushed.

"But second, I think this is a trick question," I said. "The *sun* is the closest star to the *Earth*."

"Oh, right," Faith said, knocking on her head. "I knew that."

"But what do you think Zoe is asking?"

Faith shrugged. "Go with your gut."

Leaning forward, I tapped the microphone with my finger, and then answered. "The sun. The sun is the closest star to the Earth."

Jake and his team all turned their heads simultaneously to see what Zoe was going to say.

"Correct!" Zoe shouted.

"*Gah!*" Jake screamed, flipping his table upside-down. Jumping over his flipped desk, he started running at me with eyes on fire.

Thankfully, Principal Davis stepped onto the stage before Jake could get to me.

The principal gave Jake a single look that made him back down instantly.

"Congratulations to Chase's team," Zoe smirked. "You've secured your place in the games set for tomorrow afternoon."

I sat back, exhausted from having to use my brain so much in such a small amount of time.

Faith, Gavin, and Brayden laughed, joking about what would've happened if we lost. Thank goodness we didn't have to find out.

Wednesday. 12:50 PM. The lobby.

Back in the lobby of the school, students gathered to burn about ten minutes of time until the bell rang. Earlier in the day, I had told Melvin and Slug that we were going to skip out on the wrestling room since I knew there wouldn't be much time to train.

They were both waiting patiently on the top steps of the nook, where Zoe had given the instructions before the first Spirit Week game.

"S'up, guys?" I said, dropping my book bag on the carpet next to Melvin.

"Nada," Slug said. "Are we going to train in front of all these kids? Are they going to be part of the training? Are we going to have to sneak between them and go unnoticed? First one caught loses? Oh, what if it's *you* that loses?"

"Easy there," I said, patting at the air in front of me. "We're not training out here, or at all today. I just wanted to meet you guys so I could tell you that."

Melvin sighed, but didn't really seem to mind.

Slug looked upset. "Why aren't we training? This is day three of me being in your ninja clan, and we haven't punched as many things as I thought we'd punch. Zero! Zero is the number of things that we have punched!"

"Spirit Week has kept me pretty busy," I explained and then

81

looked at Melvin. "Speaking of which, you find out anything about Wyatt?"

"Not yet, no," Melvin said. "And I can't even promise that I *will* find something. It was just a hunch."

"But did you see him in the cafeteria just now?" I asked. "He totally *owned* that quiz show!"

Melvin cocked one side of his mouth. "Yeah, but unless we find some solid evidence that he's cheating, there ain't much we can do about it."

"How about just going to the principal?" Slug said.

"I think it's best if we have a bit of that evidence I was just talking about," Melvin said. "Otherwise we're just a few kids pointing fingers."

"Do you have *any* leads at all?" I asked. "That kid on student council – I think his name is Colin? He seems like a shady dude."

"Colin?" Melvin repeated. "You think he's got somethin' to do with Wyatt winning the race?"

I nodded. "And maybe even winning the quiz show so easily too."

"Alright," Melvin replied. "I'll see what I can muster up about him, but again, I can't promise anything."

"No, I know," I said. "But at least we're trying."

Slug groaned, rocking back and forth on the top step of the nook. "Duuuudes, this is so lame! When are we going to knock some heads around?"

My eyes skimmed over my shoulder, hoping nobody heard Slug. "C'mon, man. We'll *never* knock heads around. Besides, there are other important things to deal with first."

"But why don't we just go confront Wyatt?" Slug whined.

I paused. "Because I'm pretty sure Wyatt would answer with a dropkick to my face!"

"Isn't that what we're here for though?" Slug said. "If we're ninjas, then why don't we go do *ninja* things?"

"Ninjas didn't just fight, y'know," Melvin said. I was surprised that he was siding with me. "A real ninja will choose the peaceful path every time."

"C'mon," Slug said with a half smile. "A *real* ninja would've gotten in there and baked a cake of butt kicking already."

I shook my head, confused. "That doesn't make any sense!"

Slug took a breath as he stood on his feet. "I think I'm done with this," he said flatly. "My sister was right. This is the most lame-o thing ever. I thought you were going to teach me how to kung *all* the fu, but I guess I was wrong."

I didn't know what to say, but I knew I had to say something. "Thank you for your time," I said, feeling a lump in my throat.

Slug pushed passed me and disappeared into the crowd of sixth graders waiting for the bell to ring.

Melvin remained silent, but raised his eyebrows at me. It was a "What're you gonna do?" face – a question I didn't have an answer to.

So after only three days, I had lost two out of three of my new ninjas. In my head I saw a commercial for Wyatt's red ninja clan, complete with voiceover, "*Two out of three ninjas agree – Chase Cooper's ninja clan sucks straws when compared to Wyatt's red ninja clan! The red ninja clan will also prevent gingivitis.*"

Not sure why the commercial turned all *dentist* at the end though.

Was it possible I just wasn't cut out for the ninja lifestyle? I'd had some hiccups before, but it was never as bad as the last couple weeks. The Scavengers had really kicked my social life's butt last week, but I was still feeling the bruises over a week later.

And I was really feelin' it deep in my gut. It was absolutely possible that after this week was over, I'd hang up my ninja robes for good.

Thursday. 7:44 AM. My locker.

The next morning, I took the same path as usual through the front doors of Buchanan with a half-sprint to my locker in hopes of making it to homeroom on time.

Things were eerily quiet in the hallway, but that was pretty normal when the bell was seconds away from ringing. There were always a couple kids jogging to class because they took the long way around the school for one reason or another. My reason was normally so I could chat with Faith between classes, but I had gotten to school so late that I even had to miss that – the only part of the day that made me happy.

Slamming my locker shut, I jumped back in surprise because Naomi had somehow materialized out of nowhere. Part of me wondered if she really *did* have the ability to transform into a puff of smoke like the vampire queen did in my game. Was it possible that the game was somehow based on my life? Nah...

"Heeeey," she sang as her face held the saddest smile.

I tried to act cool, but my voice cracked. "*What?*"

"I just wanted to say hi," she said. "And also give you one last, *last* chance to join The Scavengers."

For a split second, I thought about saying yes. If I were such a terrible leader, maybe I'd fit in well as a follower. But funny enough, my honor got the best of me, which was probably a good thing.

"No thanks," I said, zipping my book bag up.

"*The nail that stands up will be hammered down*," Naomi sighed, shaking her head. "Ever hear that saying?"

"No," I said.

"You're a nail that's standing up," Naomi said. "Which is why The Scavengers want to hammer you down so bad."

Just then, I felt two powerful hands grip my shoulders and yank me backward. I struggled, trying to break free, but other hands grabbed my arms and legs, lifting me into the air.

"I'm sorry," Naomi said. "I *gave* you a chance! *Two* chances even!"

"Naomi, seriously!" I begged, squirming. "This isn't even funny, dude!"

Naomi ignored my plea and kept talking. "I'm sure you've wondered why we haven't said anything to you for almost a week. Well, the truth is, we *haven't* been silent. We've been *planning*."

The three kids holding me up were strong, definitely stronger than me. No matter how hard I tried twisting around, I just couldn't. "Put me down! Let go of me!"

"Don't struggle," Naomi said. "It'll only make things worse."

"Naomi, please!" I said. "What's happening?"

One of the kids spoke from under me. "*Victor* says hello."

I couldn't see who it was that spoke, but I recognized his voice immediately. It was totally Jake. Great, right? He got booted from the red ninjas just to join The Scavengers.

But surprisingly, the fact that Jake was a Scavenger wasn't the thing that bothered me most. It was the name he uttered. "Victor?"

I heard Naomi's voice again. "He's an eighth grader here – the leader of *all* the Scavengers. And he's not too happy with you."

Then I heard the sound of duct tape getting torn from a roll. It was a sound I was familiar with because my dad used it to fix pretty much everything in the house. But the only reason someone would hear it in the hallway of a middle school was because something terrible was about to happen.

"Oh no…" I whispered.

Thursday. 8:15 AM. Still at my locker.

The bell went off at exactly 8:15, ringing loudly directly over my head. Doors to homeroom classrooms swung open as kids began flooding the hallway. I could hear the sounds of gossip and giggles come from clusters of students that walked together.

The giggles stopped for a moment when anyone saw me. But then instantly turned into loud horselaughs when they realized what they were looking at.

Humiliated, I continued to struggle, but it was impossible to move. Why? Because Naomi's friends had duct taped me to the wall. My feet were *literally* hanging off the floor.

A small crowd of students gathered around like I was some kind of freak show at a circus. I did my best to ignore the jokes and insults that were hurled in my direction.

A few of them even had their cellphones out, taking selfies with me in the background. Great, just what I needed – Internet exposure. So much for going into politics someday. I was pretty sure this meant I'd have to move to the mountains and live off the land. Y'know, lumberjackin' and stuff.

After making a duck face for her selfie, a girl smiled at me. "Thanks for the laughs," she said.

Her name was Regina. Everyone knew her as the selfie queen. Some people even called her "Duck Face," which was the

86

nickname she preferred.

"You're welcome," I said sarcastically as she walked away.

And where the heck were the teachers? How come they were always around when you didn't need them, but when you were actually in trouble, they were nowhere to be seen?

"Chase?" I heard Zoe's voice from the group of students hassling me. She pushed through the crowd, shocked at what she saw.

"Yo," I said, humiliated but trying to be cool. "Wanna hang out with me?"

Zoe choked out a laugh. "Now I know why you weren't in homeroom," she said, grabbing at a small section of duct tape around my hand. She yanked up, tearing it away from the wall.

Funny how duct tape works. I had been struggling to free myself for thirty minutes with no luck at all. Yet one tug from my cousin, and the whole thing shreds apart. That's not physics – that's magic.

I dropped to the floor, feeling my feet fill with blood again.

I felt like little needles were poking at my skin in the places where the tape had been the tightest.

"Thanks," I said. I knew I shouldn't have felt stupid, but I couldn't help it.

"Who did this?" I asked. "Wyatt?"

I held my tongue because I *almost* answered her honestly. Telling her that it was Naomi would lead to too many questions about *why* she did it. Zoe knew Naomi had been a good friend of mine, and for all I knew, Zoe still thought that.

"No," I said. "I actually don't know who it was. Some eighth graders I think."

At least *that* part was the truth.

"Seriously?" Zoe said. "Eighth graders are messing with you now?"

"Didn't you get the memo?" I asked. "*Everyone* hates me now."

"Aw," Zoe said like she was talking to a five-year-old. "You're giving yourself too much credit. No one cares."

"You don't think so?"

"I know so," she said. "That whole stunt last week with the newsletter? Everybody's over it. Sixth graders at Buchanan have the memories of a gnat. I'm sure there might be one or two that still hold a grudge, but as for ninety-nine percent of them? Already forgot about it."

"Somehow I doubt that," I said.

"It's that one percent you need to worry about," Zoe continued. "You've probably made some new enemies, but only time will tell, right?"

"Then I was just in the wrong place at the wrong time," I said, and then asked, "Do you know anyone at the school named 'Victor?'"

Zoe stopped, staring into space while thinking. "Victor? Victor... Victor..." she repeated while tapping her chin. "Y'know, I'm pretty sure there's an eighth grader named Victor. Yeah, now that I think of it, he's the dude who wears a nametag everyday."

"A nametag? Why?"

"Beats me," Zoe said. "I guess he wants people to remember his name. Is he the one that duct taped you to the lockers?"

"No," I said, feeling alright with my answer since it wasn't technically Victor that taped me up.

My cousin sighed, the kind of sigh that meant she knew I was keeping things from her, but she didn't press the issue.

Knowing that Victor wore a nametag meant avoiding him might be easier than I thought. All I had to do was keep an eye out for some weirdo with a nametag.

Zoe walked briskly down the hall. "You're lucky I was on my way to the student council room, otherwise you'd still be on display like a piece of art."

"And I thank you for that," I said, following behind. I was still finding bits of small duct tape on my clothing that I kept having to pick off.

"There's some papers I need to grab for the Buchanan Bash next week," Zoe explained. "Plus the student council room was out of cereal so I need to put an order in for a couple more boxes of it."

"You guys get cereal?" I asked.

"Sure do," Zoe said. "Since we meet super early, I thought it'd be nice to provide a light breakfast – y'know, kind of like a reward for coming to school before the sun came up. It's that new cereal, Cookie Dough Delight."

"Ew," I said. "I hate that stuff."

"*Really?*" Zoe said. "But you're such a sugar junkie! You add *milk* to your chocolate syrup!"

"I don't know how anyone likes that stuff," I said. "It's little balls of dried up cookie dough. It's like space station food."

Zoe stopped. "Again, just *another* reason for you to love it so much you'd marry it."

"The day I marry dried up balls of cookie dough is the day that I…" I paused, trying to come up with something clever. "*Die…*" I said finally.

"Wow," Zoe said frowning. "I thought you were gonna take the funny road, but instead you took the dark road. The *really, really dark* road."

Zoe turned the corner and waved goodbye.

"Any chance you'll tell me what game we're playing today?" I hollered.

"Not even a little!" Zoe shouted without looking back.

I couldn't help but laugh.

Thursday. 12:00 PM. The track.

Later that day, I met my team on the track that was down the hill from the gymnasium. Faith, Gavin, and Brayden huddled with me in a small circle as we waited for Zoe to announce what the next game was.

It was down to three teams – Wyatt's, Sophia's, and mine.

Wyatt and his team were seated at a bench on the side of the field, pointing and laughing at different kids that walked by them. Pinned to Wyatt's shirt were *two* of the bright green first place ribbons.

Sophia and her team were sitting nearby in the field, slowly plucking out single blades of grass and letting them fly away in the chilly breeze.

"It's freezing out here," Faith said with folded arms.

"Ain't so bad," Gavin commented, stuffing his hands in his pockets.

Brayden was distracted, looking over his shoulder every few seconds.

"Are you expecting someone?" I asked.

"No," Brayden said, shaking his head. "I was just seeing if Dani was out here yet."

Faith put her balled up hands against her mouth, blowing hot air into them. "Ooooo!" she crooned. "*Someone's got a*

Brayden pouted. "Do not!" he said. "Dani's just super cool, that's all. She's into really old horror movies too."

"You gonna ask her out?" Faith asked, her eyes sparkling.

As Brayden's friend, I wanted to know the exact same thing as Faith, but as a dude, I couldn't exactly ask him about it in the same way. Girls can get away with that kind of playful teasing. Dudes just make it weird.

Brayden continued scanning the field for Dani. I think he was blushing, but it might've just been the cold air. "Hey, subject change," Brayden said looking at me. "A little birdie told me you missed homeroom this morning 'cause you got taped to a wall!"

Gritting my teeth, I looked at ground. "Maybe," I said. "Maybe not."

"Maybe *yeah*," Faith joined in. "*Everyone's* talking about it. I wish I would've been there to see it."

"I'm sure the pictures will circle around the school," I groaned. "I saw enough flashes from cellphone cameras that I almost went blind."

Everyone was quiet for a moment.

I wanted so badly to tell them it was Naomi and The Scavengers, but decided not to. "Yep," I said. "That tape pulled out almost *all* my arm hair, so I guess *something* good came from it."

"Having no arm hair is good?" Brayden asked.

"It's good because Gavin won't feel so left out," I added, jokingly.

Gavin paused with an angry look on his face. "*Really? We're still joking about that?*"

Suddenly, Brayden's eyes lit up and he waved his hand. Dani was waving back from the side of the field. The two other dudes from student council were with her, puffing hot air into their hands.

Colin, the student council treasurer, watched the field carefully. I wondered if Melvin dug anything up on the kid. I'd have to remember to ask after the game.

Before Faith could go any further, Zoe's voice came from the front of the field. She was standing on one of the benches, holding a megaphone up to her face.

"Hello, everybody!" Zoe shouted. "Today's event will be a

scavenger hunt!"

A chill ran down my spine when she said "scavenger," even though it wasn't the same thing as Naomi's little band of misfits.

Mrs. Robinson, my homeroom teacher, approached my team and presented a small white envelope that was sealed with a gold metal sticker.

"The three remaining teams should receive an envelope from a teacher at any moment," Zoe continued. "Keep them sealed until I know all of you have it. After that, I'll fire off the air horn, and the scavenger hunt will begin!"

Faith took the envelope from Mrs. Robinson. Raising the envelope over her head, she blocked out the sun to try and see through it.

"Any luck?" I asked.

"Nope," Faith replied.

"Inside each envelope will be a riddle that your team will have to solve," Zoe said. "The solution is the clue to where you'll find the next envelope. To prove that you made it to each checkpoint, there will be a token to collect. Once you solve the *last* riddle, grab that last token and return to the track. Last team back is eliminated, so act fast! Oh, and there will be a surprise challenge at the end of the hunt. I'll *spare* you the details, but don't let that *strike* fear into you. Just be ready for anything!"

"What's she talkin' about?" I asked Gavin. "C'mon, man. Zoe *must've* told you *something* about this hunt, right? You guys are, like, an item or something."

Gavin sighed heavily and shrugged his shoulders. "She's good at keepin' secrets when she wants to."

Sophia and Wyatt had their envelopes and were waving them at Zoe. She lifted her air horn high over her head, but before pressing down on the button, she leaned her head over so her shoulder was covering her ear. Then with her other hand, she pushed a finger into her other ear and finally sounded the horn.

Faith wasted no time, tearing into the envelope. She pulled out the slip of paper and read the riddle. "Take my skin off, and I won't cry, but you will. What am I?"

"A monster?" Gavin joked.

Faith laughed. "But the riddle says that *we're* the ones taking the skin off."

"What do we take skin off of?" I asked, looking for Wyatt's team, but they weren't on the field anymore. They were already running back to the school. "C'mon, guys! Wyatt's team already solved the riddle!"

"No way!" Faith said. "Zoe *just* honked the horn, like, five seconds ago! We barely even opened the envelope!"

"Skin, skin, skin," Brayden repeated tapping his knuckle on his forehead. "Fried chicken? What else has skin?"

"Apples, potatoes, bananas..." Gavin said.

"Onions!" I shouted so loud that Sophia's team heard me too. "Onions don't cry when you take their skin off, but they always make *me* cry!"

"Crybaby," Brayden laughed.

Faith bolted with the envelope in her hand. "The kitchen! The next clue is somewhere in the kitchen!"

Sophia's team was sprinting across the field too, headed toward the cafeteria doors.

"Next time, don't shout the answer, okay?" Brayden said. "If we lose this, we're done for. Sophia's team will go up against Wyatt's team tomorrow, and I think we know that Wyatt will do whatever he can to win."

"Roger roger," I replied.

Brayden was right. Shouting my answer was a rookie mistake. If I wanted to keep Wyatt from creating a public red ninja clan, I was going to have to focus.

Thursday. 12:15 PM. The kitchen.

When we jumped through the doors of the kitchen, all the staff was still in the middle of cleaning up. Lunch ladies and gentlemen were spraying huge metal pans with water, blasting off any crusted cheese and meat from the meal that day.

Principal Davis and Zoe must have let the kitchen staff know there would be a bunch of sixth graders rifling through their stuff because all the adults acted as if we weren't in there.

"Onions," Faith said, searching the room with her eyes. She ran up to one of the lunch staff and shouted like a maniac. *"Where are your onions?"*

I was impressed yet fearful of the person Faith became during the competition.

The man waved his hand, gesturing to the area at the back of the kitchen.

We sprinted past everyone and turned the corner, just in time to see Wyatt rip open his second envelope over a pile of torn up onions.

"You weren't supposed to hack up the onions!" Gavin said, slipping across the floor on onion juice.

"You can't prove anything!" Wyatt said as he waved his teammates out the side door so they could solve the riddle without anyone hearing.

"He stomped on *every* onion!" I said, starting to feel the burn in my eyes.

Gavin slid around, scraping the floor with his palms, desperately searching for a second envelope. "I can't see! My eyes! They're burning!"

Faith was on the floor too, but she was holding her knees and rocking back and forth while wailing.

Sophia's team slid across the floor and crashed into the wall behind us. They grumbled together in pain, trying to figure out what just happened.

I dropped to my knees and pushed aside all the crushed onions. It was one of the most stinkiest, nastiest things I'd ever done in my life.

For the record, I've cut onions before – I'm no stranger to that. What I *was* a stranger to was rolling around in about a hundred crushed onions, feeling even more onions burst apart under the weight of my knees.

A river of tears *streamed* down my checks as I frantically searched for the second envelope. With all the tears and groaning in pain, the back of the kitchen must've looked like a roomful of sobbing sixth graders.

Suddenly I felt the sharp corner of an envelope hiding under a puddle of smashed onions.

"Got it!" I shouted, raising it high over my head while keeping my eyes shut. "Faith, take it!"

I felt a hand snatch the envelope from mine.

"Good!" I said, keeping my eyelids clenched tight. "Now help me up before you open it."

Faith's voice came from across the room. "What're you talking about? I didn't get it yet!"

"Oh-no," I said, forcing the lid of one eye open. I was fighting against my natural instinct to keep the eye closed. Through blurry vision, I saw Sophia and her team leave through the same door that Wyatt's team did. "Sophia stole it from me!"

"Get mad about it later!" Gavin sobbed. "Right now we gotta find that last envelope!"

"I'm looking! I'm looking!" I screamed, spreading my body out on the puddle of onions on the floor. "I can't breathe! It's too strong!"

"I have it!" Brayden's voice shouted.

"OMG!" Faith shouted, snatching an onion off the floor as proof that we solved the first riddle. "This was a terrible idea! *Terrible!*"

Bursting through the door, we found ourselves in the west hallway and to our surprise, a bunch of sixth graders cheering us on. It was like the race on Tuesday when students were allowed to cheer in the halls during the competition.

Brayden ripped off the top of the second envelope, and spoke. "Riddle me this," he said with a pitchy squeal.

"Quit messin' around and gimme that thing!" Gavin ordered.

Competitions can bring out the worst in friends.

Through squinted eyes, Gavin read the riddle. "What has a ring, but no finger?"

Faith opened her hand in front of her face and jokingly sang that song about single ladies.

"What the heck wears a ring with no fingers?" I asked.

"Saturn?" Brayden said. Good ol' Brayden with the sci-fi answers.

"The science room?" I suggested.

"No," Gavin said. "If Saturn were the answer, then the telescope on the roof could be the next checkpoint too. The answer has to be obvious."

"Right," I said. "Then what else has a ring, but no finger?"

"There's a ring around the bottom of the toilets," Brayden said.

"Gross," Faith snipped.

"Onion rings? A ringing bell?" I said, thinking aloud.

"A telephone rings too," Brayden said.

Like a bug bit the back of her leg, Faith jumped. "Oh! "There's a broke down payphone in the dungeon! That's *gotta* be the answer!"

"Boom!" I said.

Faith pointed her finger high into the air and shouted with a booming voice. "To the dungeon!"

Thursday. 12:26 PM. The dungeon.

A few minutes later, we were running down the steps into the lowest level of Buchanan School. It was halfway underground – not quite the basement, but also not quite at ground level.

And it was always cold and damp no matter what time of year it was, which is why most of the students referred to it as "the dungeon."

"The payphone is back by the orchestra room," Faith said, taking the lead.

I whipped my hands back and forth, trying to dry the onion juice off, but it was no use. All four of us were walking sponges of stink.

Turning the corner at the far end of the first hall, Faith stopped. "There it is," she said. "But Sophia's team is already at it."

"Any sign of Wyatt?" I asked, peeking around the corner.

"No," Faith said as she stepped out into the open.

Sophia and her team were standing next to the broken payphone, staring at the riddle from their envelope. Underneath the phone was a single envelope, which meant Wyatt's team had already come and gone.

The envelope was taped to a handset that wasn't hooked up to anything. That must've been the token we were to collect. So far we had a smooshed up onion and a telephone handset.

I took the envelope and stupidly slid my finger under the flap. It was at just the perfect angle that it gave me a paper cut. "*Knights of the round table!*" I hollered as my hand flinched and dropped the envelope. "Ohhhh, the onion juice makes it worse! It makes it *worse!*"

Faith sucked air through her teeth as she looked away.

I stared at the microscopic cut on my finger as Brayden grabbed the envelope. "I'm no use, you guys," I said, taking quick breaths. "You might have to go on without me."

"Quit yer bellyaching," Gavin said. "Brayden! Read the riddle!"

Brayden curled a creepy smile, as he spoke in the same high-pitched voice as before. "Riddle me this…"

"Just read the riddle!" I shouted, frustrated at my throbbing finger that didn't have any visible evidence of getting sliced open. How in the world were paper cuts so painful? I mean, they're so tiny that they shouldn't even exist!

"The more I dry," Brayden said, "the wetter I become."

Sophia and her entire team looked up from their envelope, about five feet away from us. It was totes obvious they were trying to "overhear" our answer.

Shuffling together as a group, we inched toward the end of the hall. Brayden grabbed the unattached handset and brought it with us.

We stopped at the corner, but could still hear shuffling feet. When I looked back at Sophia's team, they all snapped their attention to random places in the hall. Her team was still about five feet away from us even though we had moved way farther away.

"Can't even be slick about it?" Faith said, raising her head from our huddle.

"It's fine," I said, "Let's just figure this out and get going. We probably won't beat Wyatt's team, but as long as Sophia is behind us, then we're ahead."

"Agreed," Gavin said, nodding once.

"So what gets wetter the more it dries off?" Brayden asked, rolling the handset back and forth in his hands.

Everyone fell silent, trumped by the riddle.

"So as something gets drier," I said aloud. "It also gets

wetter. That doesn't make any sense."

"Wait," Faith said, snapping her fingers. "I think I... yeah, I think I got it."

We stared at her, waiting for the answer.

"Go on," I finally said.

Faith leaned closer so she could whisper quietly. "I think it's a towel."

I face-palmed myself and then whispered to my friends. "Of course! A towel *dries* things! As it dries things off, it gets wetter! Booyah!"

"I've got it," Sophia said with a deadpan voice and holding her finger up high. It was blazingly obvious that she overheard us. "The answer is a towel!"

Her team jumped to their feet and sprinted down the hall.

Faith stumbled out of our huddle. "You little cheaters!" she shouted while running away.

"Wait up!" I called out, chasing after Faith with Gavin and Brayden behind me. "Where can we find towels?"

"The janitors closet!" Faith said.

"Miss Chen-Jung ain't gonna be too happy 'bout that!" Gavin shouted.

Sophia's team dashed down the hallway and cut the corner hard. Faith slid around the corner on her shoes, able to pick up her pace again once she turned. Gavin and Brayden were bookin' it behind me.

"The main janitor's closet on the first floor is where we'll find the last clue!" Faith shouted super loudly.

Great, Faith. Why don't you let the whole school know where we're headed? At least that way they'll know why Sophia's team beat us so easily!

At the stairs of the dungeon, Sophia leapt wildly, skipping two steps between each stride. Her teammates weren't as athletic, and took to the stairs rapidly shuffling their feet. It kind of looked like they were running in place.

Faith grabbed the handrail, and stomped her foot on the first step, but came to a complete stop after that.

"What're you waiting you for?" I said, jumping onto the staircase, clearing three steps.

Faith pushed her finger against her tightened lips. With her other hand, she pointed straight up.

The sound of Sophia and her team running desperately to the janitor's closet on the first floor rumbled through the brick walls.

Gavin and Brayden stopped behind Faith at the bottom of the steps, clutching their stomachs, trying to catch their breath.

I sighed, throwing my hands in the air. "What?" I asked.

About three seconds later, the stomping footsteps faded out, which meant Sophia's team was pretty much out of earshot.

Faith took a deep breath, smiling. Jogging up the staircase, she checked the lobby to see if it was clear. Besides a few students watching the scavenger hunt, it was nearly empty.

"The towels *aren't* in the janitor's closet," Faith said.

"What?" I asked, confused. "Wait... *what?*"

"All Sophia's going to find is a bunch of mops and cleaning supplies," Faith explained. "The envelope probably wanted us to go to the locker rooms."

"Whoa," Brayden said. "That's brilliant! You sent Sophia's team on a wild turkey hunt!"

"Wild goose chase," Gavin corrected.

"Sure did," Faith said proudly as she sped her pace. "But we should keep moving. It won't take them long to realize there aren't any towels in there. And even less time if Miss Chen-Jung is in room."

Together, we ran through the lobby and into the hallway where the entrances to the locker rooms were. I looked back and forth between the women's restroom door and the men's restroom door.

"So which one do we go into?" I asked.

"Do you think it matters?" Gavin asked. "This is the last token so I bet any towel will do."

"You got a point," Faith said, pushing against the women's locker room door, but it didn't budge. "Well, nevermind then. Since this door is locked, we *have* to go into the men's locker room."

"Um," I said to Faith, hesitating. "Maybe you should just go to the track and meet us out there."

"Nuh-uh!" Faith snipped. "We're all in this together! We're a team and we do everything as a team!"

"Don't say I didn't warn you," I gulped, pushing the door to the men's locker room open.

Gavin and Brayden chuckled at the face Faith made when the putrid smell of the locker room hit her nose.

Pouting, she said, "What *is* that? It smells like a wet dog just rolled around in some wet socks... and then *pooped* all over the place!"

Suddenly, Sophia's voice echoed down the hallway. "There! You think you're so smart, huh? I *knew* there weren't any towels in the janitor's closet! I just wanted you to *think* I didn't know!"

Faith gasped. Pinching her nose and shaking her head, she dove into the men's locker room. Brayden, Gavin, and I followed her lead.

Thursday. 12:35 PM. The last token.

Inside the dark locker room, we made our way down different aisles separated by gym lockers. We split up so we could find the towels we needed to win the race.

The door to the entrance swung open and creaked shut. Sophia and her team were also in there.

"Come out, come out, wherever you are," Sophia's voice eerily sang.

I heard Faith's voice complain. "Why are *all* the floors wet? Like, every step I take is in a puddle! *What* am I stepping on?"

Some of Sophia's teammates complained and groaned about the smell too.

I turned the corner, surprised by someone's shadow, but it just turned out to be Brayden.

"Any luck?" he asked.

I shook my head. "Normally they're just sitting out on the table in front of the coach's office, but I don't see any of them at all."

"I bet Wyatt hid them," Brayden said.

My heart sunk because he was probably right.

"So if you were Wyatt, where would you hide them?" I whispered.

I heard footsteps walking slowly from elsewhere in the

locker room. Sophia's team was still creeping around somewhere.

Gavin and Faith stepped around the corner, joining us when they noticed we were there.

"Wyatt probably hid the towels," Brayden said, nodding.

"Course he did," Gavin said. "Sounds like our Wyatt."

"Don't call him 'our Wyatt,'" Faith snipped.

"We just can't think of where the towels would be though," Brayden added.

And then a light bulb switched on in my head. "They're probably in his locker," I said, looking at what row we were in, which just happened to be the same one that Wyatt's locker was in.

Brayden spun around and looked through the metal grate of Wyatt's locker. "Yep," he said. "There they are. Two perfectly folded bright white towels."

"Any of you got a locker key?" Gavin asked hopelessly. "Or better yet, maybe one of you knows his combination?"

Faith ran her fingers along the metal grate of the locker, studying it carefully not with her eyes, but with her sense of touch.

Then her hand stopped, and she blinked. Stepping back, she brought her elbow up and rammed it into the bottom corner of Wyatt's locker, making the door flip wide open.

Gavin, Brayden, and I stared at her with our jaws dropped.

"I learned that little move back in the war," she joked.

Brayden snatched the towel on top and grabbed the door to the locker. He started to shut it, but I stopped him.

"Wait!" I said. "Leave it open for Sophia."

"But we'll win for sure if she can't get to the last towel!" Brayden said.

I shook my head. "If we shut it, then we're just like Wyatt."

Brayden nodded obediently. Then he ran to the exit of the locker room with Gavin by his side.

Narrowing my eyes at Faith, I stared at her for a second, hoping she might give in and just *tell* me she was the white ninja. When she smiled cluelessly back at me, I asked, "You *are*, *aren't* you?"

"I'm what?" Faith asked, smiling. "No idea what you're talking about it."

As she jogged down the aisle to the exit, Sophia's team rounded the corner and spotted the last towel in Wyatt's locker.

"Grab it!" she commanded her hipster teammates.

I ran toward the exit of the gym, jumping through the door with Sophia's entire team running behind me.

Outside, my friends were standing at the edge of the parking lot, staring at the track at the bottom of the long hill. Most of the sixth graders had made it back outside and were cheering for the last two teams to finish the hunt.

Wyatt's team was already resting on the benches at the side of the track.

"Why aren't you guys going?" I asked, skidding across the gravel to a stop.

Gavin pointed toward the track. "Because of those."

At the bottom of the hill were two sets of oversized bowling pins standing right next to each other. They were set up in the typical fashion with ten pins that made a triangle which were aimed back at us.

At our feet was an empty book bag with a skateboard next to it. About ten feet away from us was another book bag and skateboard.

I wasn't surprised to see two lines in the grass that led from the parking lot all the way down to another set of pins that had been knocked over. Wyatt's team must've ridden the first skateboard.

"Oh," I said. Doing my best "Zoe" impersonation, I spoke while bobbing my head back and forth. "*I'll* spare *you the details, but don't let that* strike *fear into you.* Nice."

Sophia's team burst through the exit of the men's locker room. They were a bunch of confused hipsters, staring at us like, "*Why are you guys still up here?*"

Immediately Sophia's eyes darted to the skateboard that was next to us, and then toward the bowling pins down on the track.

Like a boss, she shouted, "Human bowling!"

I looked at my team. "Who's gonna do this?"

All eyes were back on me, but nobody answered. It didn't take a genius to know what they were thinking though.

Sophia took the empty bag and stuffed the three scavenger hunt tokens into it.

"Fine," I said, not wanting to waste another second. I grabbed the bag off the skateboard and slammed all three of our

105

tokens inside the canvas. "I'll do it!"

Brayden and Faith took a step back to give me room. Sitting on the skateboard, I stuck my arms through the straps of the book bag and stared at the pins down the hill.

"Ready?" Gavin asked as he put his hands on my back.

"Nope!" I said, gripping the sides of the skateboard.

Sophia's team pushed against her back as she rode the skateboard.

"Too bad!" Gavin shouted as he forced me forward. As we gained speed down the hill, he said, "In case you die, I just want you to know you've been an awesome bro!"

Feeling his hands release me, my skateboard flew forward. "*Thaaaaaaaaank youuuuuuu!*" I shouted through my teeth.

The hill to the track was surprisingly bumpy. When you walk along the ground, you hardly ever realize what kind of lumps and junk there are in the dirt.

Sophia and I were neck and neck, racing toward our own set of pins at the bottom of the hill on the track. The line of students started about halfway down the path on both sides of us.

The farther down the hill we rode, the faster we went. For a second, I was afraid that I'd shoot back in time if my skateboard got up to 88 miles per hour, like in that one movie my dad loves.

From the corner of my eye, I saw Sophia clutching at her skateboard. She was close enough that I could hear her teeth chattering as she hummed through them.

Down on the track, I saw Zoe with an excited smile on her face. Principal Davis was standing by her side with a grin of his own. Wyatt and his team looked unamused and bored, waiting on the bench for the hunt to be over.

Everything was looking pretty good as my skateboard pulled forward by a few feet. That is, until I felt Sophia's foot scrape my back. When I looked behind me, I saw that she was right on my tail, swinging one foot back and forth, trying to get me to fall off my skateboard.

"*Are you crazy?*" I shouted, feeling my board wobble underneath me.

She didn't answer as she continued to swing her foot at me. Every time I looked back at her, I expected to see an angry girl staring daggers at me, but it was far more terrifying than that. She had *no emotion* on her face whatsoever. Blank and devoid of human expression – like a robot sent from the future to "take care of me" because I would grow up to be the leader of the resistance.

My skateboard shook violently under my butt as the wheels dug into the dirt. The cold air stung my cheeks as I leaned forward, trying to keep my face from getting a grass burn. Sophia's foot swung at me again.

"*Stop that!*" I shouted, but it was too late.

I felt the front of my board dig into the dirt, stopping me instantly. No wait, that's not right – it stopped *the skateboard* instantly. I, on the other hand, shot forward like I was just fired out of a cannon.

Sailing through the air, everything was peaceful and silent. I even had enough time to see that Sophia had also tripped herself up because her skateboard smashed into mine.

And just like me, she was flying over the grass… coming straight at me with eyes burning red. Shooting both hands forward, I watched in horror as her skin changed from a pale fleshy color to a super shiny liquid metal.

WHAT THE WHAT???

I tried to land on the ground, but I was still flying too fast, unable to do anything but watch as the psycho hipster gained on me.

Her fingers suddenly morphed into long metallic blades that she snipped toward me, the same way everyone does with scissors before using them. Somehow she was able to speed up, gaining on me rather quickly.

Dirt and grass flew everywhere as she used her machete fingers to tear into the earth, nearly at my feet as we both flew through the air.

"It's no use! The machines have already won!" she shouted, pointing her sword finger at me. "Give up now, Chase!"

I raised my fist. "Never!" I screamed.

The back of my head thumped against the grass, and all the chaos ended instantly.

When I opened my eyes, I was staring at the principal's face. Gavin, Brayden, and Faith were standing next to him.

Humongous white bowling pins were spread out around me too.

"Never what?" Zoe asked, kneeling next to me.

My fist was still over my head. "Um…" I said, lowering my arm and sitting up, slowly realizing Sophia's liquid metal pursuit of me was just a bizarre dream I had from probably blacking out.

Sophia was still at the spot where she had tried to kick me halfway down the hill.

"What happened?" I asked.

"You torpedoed off your board and rolled into the bowling pins," Gavin explained. "After Sophia kicked your skateboard, she lost balance and fell on the hill."

"Huh…" I grunted. "So… did we beat her?"

Zoe nodded rapidly, beaming a smile that made the air feel less chilly.

I breathed a sigh of relief as I stood. In her lame attempt to get me to spill, Sophia made herself biff. I guess I couldn't complain though – her little stunt was what secured our spot for the last game.

Everyone on my team was celebrating with cheers and high fives. Even Zoe, who wasn't on the team, joined in. It felt good to make it through the second to the last competition for Spirit Week, but I knew I wasn't going to be happy until the last game of the week was over.

Thursday. 12:55 PM. The cafeteria.

Back in the lobby, I was standing near the entrance of the cafeteria, leaning against the wall and minding my own business. Melvin was supposed to meet me there after the competition to go over some more ninja stuff, but I couldn't find him anywhere.

With my luck, he probably decided to quit too.

The sixth graders were scattered pretty evenly between the lobby and the cafeteria. Those who didn't feel like standing were sitting at lunch tables.

I stepped up to the tinted glass window and peered through. Maybe Melvin had already gone into the cafeteria before I got there.

"Dreaming of what it's like having friends?" Wyatt's voice asked from behind me.

I turned around. Wyatt was standing at the entrance of the cafeteria with the rest of his team. "What?" I asked.

Wyatt pointed at the glass window. "I saw you," he said snidely. "Creepily watching other people and wishing you were part of their group."

"That's not—" I said.

But Wyatt cut me off, sounding a lot like a baby. "Are too! Are too, are too, are too!"

His team chuckled and bumped fists, commenting on how

~~Wyatt just burned me.~~

I nodded with eyes half shut. "Okay."

"You should just forfeit the last game now," Wyatt suggested. "It'll save you the humiliation of defeat. I mean, I know you're used to it by now, but I seriously think you have a problem. Like, maybe you're addicted to it?" His face softened with a genuinely concerned look. "Chase, are you *addicted* to being the school loser? Because if so, I can help you that."

Wyatt was beginning to get on my nerves. Actually, Wyatt had never been *off* my nerves. "Oh yeah? How can you help?" I asked.

"My best advice is to have you quit the games cold turkey," he said super seriously as he stepped closer to me. And then he slugged my shoulder, not in the "let's fight" kind of way, but in the "hey there, kiddo," way. With a sad smile, he said, "Just give up."

I stared back at the short boy before me, feeling my insides twist out of shape. He was good at saying the perfect thing to make me upset.

Wyatt's team managed to come in first every time, which could've meant two things – first, that he was somehow gaming the system to win, or second, his team was actually *good* at the Spirit Week games and were legit in how they played.

Either way, I felt the crushing weight of defeat on my shoulders. There was a huge part of me that *did* want to back out now. The last game was less than a day away, and with Wyatt's record, my odds for winning were pretty slim.

So I continued to stare at Wyatt, who was starting to raise his eyebrows at me like he was waiting for me to say something.

The twins, Gidget and Slug, had suddenly stepped forward too, wondering what was going on. They looked back and forth between Wyatt and me as we stared each other down.

If my team competed in the last game, we might lose in front of the entire school. Wyatt would win, and he'd get his public ninja clan. If that happened, then there's no telling what kind of evil schemes he'd be able to get away with.

But if I quit, would my friends even blame me for it? I could just disappear into the sea of other students and float my way through the rest of school until graduation. The more I thought about it, the better it sounded.

No more getting singled out. No more ninja clan to worry about. No more attention. No more humiliation or embarrassment. No more *anything*.

"Dude," Wyatt said, snapping me away from my thoughts. "It's been like a minute and half. Are you going to say something or just keep staring?"

I paused. "Nothing," I said. "I'm not going to say anything."

"Good," Wyatt said, turning around. He raised his hand, snapping his fingers at his teammates. They obediently followed their master through the cafeteria door. Wyatt reached into his back pocket and pulled out a crumpled bit of yellow paper, tossing it into the garbage next to the entrance.

At the exact same time, I saw Melvin step out of the cafeteria doors. His arm was slung around a small pile of textbooks that also had his notepad on top. He was so busy scribbling some chicken scratch onto the paper that he didn't even see Wyatt.

When they collided, Wyatt freaked.

"Why don't you watch where you're going?" Wyatt shouted like a maniac, throwing his arms into the air.

Melvin looked up from his notepad, confused. "What? I'm sorry, I was just—"

Immediately Wyatt snatched Melvin's books from him and slammed them into the garbage can. Then he turned around and continued his tirade. "You almost made me fall! Is *that* what you wanted? Were you trying to do it on purpose?"

Melvin stuttered, unsure of what to say.

And me? I was already dashing to get between Wyatt and Melvin. I didn't have a plan, but I knew I couldn't waste time trying to think of one.

Stepping between the two boys, I smiled at Wyatt. "It was an accident, alright?"

Wyatt stepped forward, pushing at my shoulders. "C'mon, man. Gimme a reason!"

"I'll give you a reason to walk away," I said, realizing *everyone* in the lunchroom was staring. "Because you and I have a showdown tomorrow, and if you throw out any punches, you'll get disqualified in a heartbeat. You might as well not even show up to the game if that happens."

Wyatt took a breath, slowly leaning back. "C'mon, guys," he said, gesturing to his team. "These dandelions aren't worth the trouble anyway."

As Wyatt and his squad walked away, I reached into the garbage can and grabbed Melvin's stuff, along with bits of trash that had stuck to his books.

"Did he just call us dandelions?" Melvin asked.

"Yeah," I said, doing my best to wipe off the nasty mixture of mashed potatoes and spaghetti sauce from Melvin's textbooks. "He says weird things like that *all* the time. Sometimes they make sense, but most of the time they don't."

"Thanks," Melvin said, taking his books from me. His notepad was still in one piece, but was soaked in corn juice. "Sick."

Melvin and I sat at one of the empty tables near the stage.

"So I'm still looking into the whole thing about Wyatt winning these games so easily," Melvin said, "but I'm not coming up with anything. It looks like he's just *really* good at leading his team."

Grunting, I leaned forward, burying my face in my hands. "I was afraid of that."

"Which makes what I have to say even harder for me,"

Melvin choked out.

I peeked between my fingers, already knowing what he was gonna say. "What?"

Melvin wasn't the kind of kid who skirted around a subject. He was a straight-to-the-point kind of guy, which was why I respected him. "I quit," he said.

"Figures," I sighed. "But I just saved your butt back there!"

"And I appreciate that," he replied politely. "But I just don't think this whole ninja thing is for me."

"So that's it then? You're just done?"

"Well, yeah," Melvin said. "That's what *quitting* means."

A knot formed in my throat. "Welp, that does it. Worst. Ninja. Leader. Ever."

Melvin made an "*are you serious?*" face. Then he stood from the table. "Thanks for helping me out with Wyatt back there. I'll definitely be rooting for your team tomorrow. Good luck."

He wasn't sarcastic when he said it.

I rested my chin on the cold lunch table and watched the other students talking and laughing with each other. There was so much that happened behind the scenes at this school, and I was beginning to envy everyone who didn't have a clue about any of it.

Friday. 7:35 AM. Outside.

"So he just up and quit? Like that?" Brayden asked, sitting on the opposite side of the bench I was on.

We were outside, wasting some time before going into the school. The sun was bright and the air was cold and dry. Perfect weather if you asked me, which you didn't, so I'm just sayin'.

"He did," I said to Brayden. "So it's just down to you and me."

Brayden nodded slowly, watching the other kids gather at the front doors of Buchanan School.

"Unless you're quitting now too," I half-joked.

"Course not," Brayden said. "There's no way I can go back to normal life after being in your ninja clan. You know how *boring* it would be? *Normal* school? *Barf!*"

"Hey, guys," a boy's voice said as his shadow crept toward our feet.

When I looked up, I saw Brody Valentine standing over me. He was someone in the school that I considered a friend, but really knew nothing about. We had zero classes together and occasionally saw each other in the hallways.

The only reason I had ever talked to the kid was because Faith and Zoe were friends with one of his friends named Maddie. So we were basically friends because our *friends* were friends.

Make sense?

"What's up, dude?" I asked Brody.

"Typical things, y'know. Same stuff, different day," he said, breathing out small puffs of fog in the frigid air.

Unsure of how to carry the conversation, I nodded. "Cool," and then repeated it slower. "*Coooooooooool.*"

Brody laughed, looking like he shared the exact awkward feeling I had. "So Maddie told me—" he stopped. "You guys know Maddie?"

Brayden and I nodded together.

"Well, she told me you might be having a rough couple weeks," Brody said nervously. "So I know this might be weird, but if you ever need anything, just let me know. Seriously, anything."

I wasn't sure why, but that simple act of reaching out to me was enough to brighten my morning, even if it was just a tiny bit.

It was such a small gesture from Brody, but it meant *so* much to me, like others actually *cared* about how I was feeling. I made sure to take a mental note about what I was thinking – be cool to *everyone, all* the time, because everyone needs it even if it doesn't seem like they do.

I should put that on a t-shirt.

Finally, I spoke up. "Thanks, man, but I'm good."

"Alright," he said, puffing out his chest. "Well, the offer still stands, kay? For both you guys."

Brayden smiled. "Cool."

I nodded.

Brody went through the front doors of the school.

Brayden and I stood from our bench and spent another minute outside, breathing in the refreshing cold air of the morning.

Friday. 12:05 PM. The hallways.

Half a day later, I was outside the gymnasium doors with Zoe and Faith. Gavin and Brayden were already inside the gym waiting for the games to begin even though we still had about ten minutes until the last assembly started for Spirit Week.

"Any chance you'll tell me what the final game for today is?" I asked my cousin, hoping that she'd actually give in and confess.

"You only have to wait, like, ten more minutes, and you'll find out along with everyone else!" Faith said.

"I know, right?" Zoe huffed, folding her arms. "You've been trying all week to get special treatment just 'cause you're my cousin. Not a chance in *heck*, son!"

"The school year isn't over," I said. "There's still plenty of time."

Zoe and Faith laughed.

Sixth graders pushed past us, clearing out the halls and entering the gym. No sign of Wyatt's team yet, but that didn't mean much. They were around.

Finally, I heard Principal Davis give some announcements about sitting space and how everyone needed to be clear of the center of the gym.

And then I saw it. A flash of red from the corner of my eye.

118

It was so quick that I wouldn't even have noticed it if I were a regular student.

But I wasn't a regular student. I was a ninja.

The red blur was all the way down the hall. If the blur had been *any* other color, I would've ignored it, but because it was red, I had an inkling that it might be someone from the red ninja clan.

I folded my arms and stared at the end of the hallway as Faith and my cousin blah blah blahed back and forth to each other.

The flash of blur happened again, but this time I saw exactly what was going on. It *was* one of Wyatt's red ninjas chasing after another student. I think I even heard the faint sound of someone shouting for help.

I turned back to Zoe. "Hey," I said quickly. "You guys head in there. I have to, um, y'know, bathroom break." I tend to say too much when bending the truth, which was why I added, "Hope there's a plunger in there! Am I right?"

My brain screamed in my skull. *Why would you say that?*

Zoe and Faith both looked horrified.

"Okaaaaay," Zoe said. "TMI, but good luck with that."

"Thanks," I said as I lowered my head like an embarrassed dog. "I'll catch up."

"Well, hurry up!" Faith said. "The last game's gonna start soon."

"And you don't want Wyatt to accidentally win if you don't show up," Zoe said. "If the *entire* team isn't there, then it's an automatic forfeit."

"I get it," I said, nodding. "Now please, just head in and I'll be right behind you."

Zoe said something else, but I missed it. All I knew was that she was a little annoyed that I was being pushy, but I didn't have any time to waste! The red ninjas were up to no good, and I *had* to check it out!

After the gymnasium doors shut, I found myself alone in the hallways. Glancing down both sides of me, I double-checked to make sure I really *was* alone.

I reached into the hood of my sweatshirt where I kept my ninja mask. Gripping it with my fingers, I pulled it down over my face.

It was *go* time.

Friday. 12:15 PM. The empty hallway.

At the end of the hall, I poked my head around the corner before diving out into the open. The coast was clear, which was kind of a bummer since I was *trying* to find someone.

Just then I heard the sound of a girl's voice shout for help again. It came from one of the empty rooms down the hall.

Without waiting another second, I dashed to the room where noise was coming from, but to my surprise, there was nobody there.

"Uh, hello?" I said, feeling sick to my stomach that I might have just walked into a trap. At that point in my life, it could've been anyone setting me up – the red ninja clan, The Scavengers, Jake and his wolf pack.

The voice came again from one of the rooms behind me. "Help me!"

I spun in a circle, confused because I swore I had heard the shout coming from the room I was looking in.

"What's going on?" I asked aloud, carefully stepping across the hallway to the next open door.

Without warning, a girl jumped out of the dark room. I freaked, throwing my arms in the air to try and protect my face from getting smacked.

The girl smashed into me, sending us both to the floor tumbling. When the dust cleared, I looked at my attacker. It was Brayden's friend, Dani.

The look on her face was terrified as she stared at me, but then I remembered I was wearing a ninja mask.

"What's going on?" I asked, my voice muffled from the black cloth over my face. "Are you okay?"

Dani's hands were shaking as she looked past me. "Them!"

I didn't need to turn around to know there was probably a boatload of red ninjas standing behind me. But I did anyway.

In the doorway were about ten red ninjas, arms folded, eyes piercing, and legs uh… standing.

The red ninja at the front of the group knocked his knuckles together. "Look what the cat dragged in."

I jumped to my feet, helping Dani off the floor. "Run! I'll take care of this!"

Through tears in her eyes, she looked at me nodding. Then she dashed down the hall without saying another word.

Placing my feet firmly on the carpeted floor, I clenched my fists, holding them at my side. Nodding my head once at the red ninjas, I growled. "Let's dance."

All ten of the red ninjas looked amongst themselves, confused.

Just so you know, that was all part of my plan – confuse the red ninjas by making them think I was up for a fight. In their confusion, I would take off like a bolt of lightning, which is *exactly* what I did.

I was halfway down the hall before they noticed I had escaped.

"Ha!" I shouted. "Suckers!"

At that moment, a second group of red ninjas jumped out of another room in front of me.

"Whoops," I muttered, skidding to a stop.

So there I was in the hallway, two herds of red ninjas wearing blue jeans on both sides of me closing in quickly. I kept whipping my head back and forth between the two herds, trying my best to come up with some kind of awesome ninja plan.

I ran to one of the empty classrooms nearby, twisting the door handle. Of course, it was locked, because my luck wouldn't have it any other way.

Both groups of ninjas were about ten feet away on both sides of me. This was going to be bad. Like, *bad* bad. Like, *more* than getting duct taped to the wall bad.

I leaned against the door, feeling a little dizzy because it felt like I was having a bad dream.

Wait, I thought. Maybe I *was* having a bad dream!

I shut my eyes and banged the back of my head against the locked classroom door. The thud traveled through my body and looked like it traveled across the floor because all the red ninjas flinched when they saw me do it.

Okay, brain. Time to wake up… like, any second now.

But the red ninjas continued their approach. Some of the fluorescent lights overhead had burned out, which cast eerie shadows of the encroaching ninjas along the floor and walls.

Darnit. I was about to get my butt handed to me, and I even gave them a head start by bruisin' up my noggin.

I inhaled deeply, preparing for what was about to go down.

And then the door clicked.

My heart nearly leapt out of my chest.

I jumped forward as the door flew wide open. There, standing in the doorway, was the white ninja.

"Come on!" the white ninja said with a husky voice, obviously trying to disguise their real voice.

I did as the white ninja commanded and jumped into the classroom.

The white ninja slammed the door shut, turning the lock.

"Thanks," I said, looking for another way out. The only door in the room was the one we had just locked. Along the back of the classroom was a set of tall closets built into the wall. On the counters were mixing bowls and spatulas. We were in the home economics room.

"Don't thank me yet," the white ninja said.

"Wait, how'd you get in here if that's the only way in?" I asked.

"I dove in here and locked the door when I saw you getting chased," the white ninja said. "Let's just say it's in my best interest to look after you."

"I totally know it's you!" I said with a huge smile under my mask. It *had* to be Faith, right? I mean, all signs pointed to yes, didn't they? "You think you're fooling me, but you're not!"

The white ninja stepped farther into the room, scanning the sides for an exit, fully ignoring me.

"Don't bother," I said. "There's no other way out. We're stuck."

"Not good," the white ninja growled. "Stupid. Stupid, stupid, stupid!"

"Don't be so hard on yourself!" I said. "Those red ninjas can't touch us as long as that door remains locked."

As if the door had been waiting for its time to shine, the latch flipped, unlocking with a clunking sound.

"Awesome," I said.

The door creaked open, I watched as all the red ninjas stepped through, blocking our only way to escape.

"I'm not sure what you're planning," I said. "But you're going to be pretty disappointed if it's a fight you're looking for."

The red ninjas parted, creating a path for someone to walk

down. It was Wyatt. Of course it was Wyatt. It was *always* Wyatt.

"Then it's a good thing nobody's looking for a fight," Wyatt sneered as he patted at all three of his first place ribbons pinned to his shirt. "Isn't that right, Chase?"

I didn't care that Wyatt used my real name. Anyone who was a ninja in this school knew who other ninjas were. If there was someone in the room who *wasn't* a ninja, I know he wouldn't have said my name. It's like the only integrity that kid had.

In order to show Wyatt and the red ninjas that we weren't looking for a fight, the white ninja and I sat on our knees, placing our hands on our thighs.

"Shouldn't you be getting ready for the last game?" I asked through my mask.

"I would ask you the same question," he replied. He turned quickly, I think on purpose so his ribbons would flourish a bit, and faced the white ninja. "And you... you've been something of a mystery this past month, haven't you?"

The white ninja said nothing, but I could tell they were getting nervous. Their chest was moving up and down quickly, taking rapid breaths.

Wyatt leaned closer to the white ninja's mask. "Who *are* you under there?"

"Leave her alone!" I snapped. I hated that Faith had been caught up in this mess. It rocked me to my core – if it weren't for me, she'd be in the gymnasium, safe and sound.

With a smile, Wyatt stood tall.

I exhaled slowly, relieved that he was going to leave her alone.

But instantly, he clutched the top of her ninja mask and pulled it off her face.

In that moment, my brain completely fizzled out. I felt like maybe I was seeing things, because *Faith* was supposed to be the one under the mask... but it wasn't.

It was Zoe.

Friday. 12:19 PM. Prisoners in the classroom.

My cousin remained perfectly still, resting on her knees with her hands on her thighs. She stared at the floor, super angry, but unflinching.

"No stinkin' way," Wyatt whispered, holding back the kind of laughter that comes when you're downright shocked. I knew because I felt the exact same way.

Wyatt looked at me and said something, but I had no idea what it was. All I could do was stare at my cousin who was decked out in a white ninja costume. Somewhere in my brain, there was an error message that continued to blink, "Application not responding."

"Wow," Wyatt said at last, tossing the white ninja mask at my cousin's feet. "Ya think ya know a gal."

"You don't know *anything* about me," Zoe whispered.

Wyatt laughed. "I know you're the president! I know that if word gets out that you're running around with your cousin dressed as ninjas, you'd lose your position in office! Ya like apples? How's about *them* apples?"

Zoe didn't say a word.

"This is just *too* good," Wyatt said. "That's fine. I'll figure out how to deal with all this after I win the final game."

"The game won't start unless Zoe's there," I said with

127

confidence.

Wyatt shook his head. "Not true," he said. "Principal Davis will simply take the lead when he sees that Zoe's gone."

Zoe looked at me. "He's right. The game will still go on."

"But it doesn't matter much anyway," Wyatt continued as he turned to me, "because when Davis finds out that someone is missing from *your* team, then you automatically forfeit."

"That's why I'm down here," I said in horrible understanding. "You never intended there to be a fight."

"Oh, of course not," Wyatt said. "I *knew* I could count on you to be honorable and take your place in the land of defeat. I *knew* you'd rather sit here and lose the game instead of throwing punches."

I wasn't sure if I *hated* that Wyatt was right, or if it was actually *cool* that he was.

"Pretty brilliant plan, right?" the leader of the red ninjas gloated. "I mean, either way, you lose! If you decide to fight your way out of this, you get suspended from school, which is an automatic disqualification. And if you decide to be noble, you'll just sit here until my red ninjas allow you to leave, which will be long after you've already been disqualified because of your absence. Man!" Wyatt said through his clenched teeth. "I. Am. Brilliant!"

"Gross," Zoe whispered.

Wyatt laughed at Zoe's comment. "Get comfortable, sugar, because you're gonna be in here until *after* the assembly." He looked at Zoe's white ninja uniform. "Why white? You stick out like a... well, like a white ninja."

"Black isn't my color," Zoe replied coolly.

"Red might suit you," Wyatt said.

"Pfft!" Zoe huffed. "Haven't you heard? White is the new black."

"Sure," Wyatt chuckled quietly. "I'll call you when there's a snowstorm."

"Like red is better?" Zoe asked, arching her brow.

"Better than white," Wyatt said like a baby.

"Is not."

"Is too."

"Nuh-uh."

"Uh-huh."

"*Nuh-uh!*"

"*Uh-huh!*"

I seriously had to bite the inside of my cheek to keep myself from laughing at how childish my cousin was acting.

"Whatever!" Wyatt shouted. "I don't have time for this!"

Zoe and I watched Wyatt cut a path through his red ninjas again. Before he stepped out the door, he turned. "You should've just given up, Chase."

With that, Wyatt disappeared into the hallway.

Most of the red ninjas went with him. The leftovers stood with their arms folded right inside the entrance, poking their head out every few seconds to make sure no one was coming.

"So..." I sang, a little amused. "Look at *you!*"

"Don't even," Zoe said.

"Why didn't you just tell me?" I asked.

"Because," Zoe said, rolling her eyes. "I'm *not* the white

ninja. You already knew I wasn't interested in all this."

I felt my eyebrows squeeze together as they lowered on my forehead. "Um, what?"

"You heard me."

"Except that you're right next to me wearing some white ninja robes."

"Faith asked me to do this as a favor for her," Zoe said. "And since we're besties, I couldn't say no. That and the fact that you're my cousin and needed my help."

"I *knew* it!" I said through my mask. "Faith *is* the white ninja!"

Zoe made a "duh-doy" face. "She told me you already knew."

"Kind of," I said. "I mean, yeah, totally. I totes knew it was her, like, the *whole* time. Super totes. I know, right?"

"So…" Zoe said. "What's the plan, boss?"

I looked at the red ninjas at the door, and then back at my cousin. "I don't have a plan this time," I admitted. "I think it's over. All of it."

Zoe's face shifted from worried to angry. "Are you serious?"

I pulled my ninja mask off my face, feeling the cool air touch my cheeks. "These last couple weeks have a been a nightmare for me."

"Well, I'm not gonna say I *didn't* notice you acting all paranoid," Zoe said.

"I just don't know how much longer I can keep going," I said honestly, only because she was family. If it were anyone else, I probably wouldn't have said anything. "And now look at me. Sitting in an empty classroom while a couple of red ninjas keep me from leaving all because their leader wants to win the last game during Spirit Week so he can make his ninja clan a public club. I'm probably the most horrible leader that ever existed."

Zoe sighed, looking angrier. "Pretty sure there's been worse."

"I don't mean it like that," I said. "I mean, I've pretty much failed to be a good leader."

Finally, Zoe's face turned red. "Would you stop having a pity party for yourself?"

130

"Huh?" I grunted, confused.

From my place in the classroom, I heard footsteps as they thumped down the hallway. There was a dark blur in front of the door, and then the sound of footsteps squeaking to a stop. Melvin's face peeked around the corner.

Maybe the universe was cutting me a break! When Melvin saw Zoe and me, he'd go back and find help!

"Dude!" he said as he bounced through the door, holding a crinkly yellow envelope over his head. He wasn't wearing his suit jacket, and his shirt was untucked and disheveled like he had been working all night. "I've got brain popping news!"

"Melvin, wait!" I shouted. "Don't come in here!"

Melvin didn't listen, taking quick steps to reach me. "I have proof that Wyatt cheated! He knew all the locations for the scavenger hunt *and* all the answers for the quiz show!"

The door to the classroom slammed shut.

Melvin spun around, shocked. "Uh-oh."

My hope that he would save the day petered out.

"Yep," one of the ninjas said with arms folded. I could tell it was a girl under the mask from the way her voice sounded. She pointed at the spot between Zoe and me. "Sit."

Melvin raised his hands as if he were surrendering. "Sure thing," he said, taking a knee. "Not a problem."

I stared at the floor, not wanting to say a word. It was possible that the gymnasium was already celebrating Wyatt's victory. Being at the other end of the school, I really had no way of telling.

"What were you doing down here anyway?" Zoe asked. "Shouldn't you be in the gym?"

"Shouldn't *you?*" Melvin snipped. "You're the gosh darn president!" He turned his head to look at me. "And you'd best get down to the gym unless you're planning to forfeit!"

I said nothing.

Melvin's face softened. He understood. "So that's that, huh?"

Again, I said nothing.

"What kind of proof do you have that Wyatt cheated?" Zoe asked.

Melvin tossed the wrinkled yellow envelope he was carrying onto the floor. "It's all right there," he said.

Zoe's eyes followed the envelope as it fell to the carpet. "What's *that?*"

"That," Melvin said, "was the thing that Wyatt threw into the trash yesterday."

"The trash?" I repeated.

Melvin smiled. "Yep. Wyatt tossed it out just before I bumped into him. Remember that? And then he dumped all my books in with it. Well, when you grabbed my textbooks, you accidentally grabbed his envelope too."

"What's in it?"

Melvin paused, his smile growing more satisfied. "Oh, nothin' much, except for the exact locations of each token for the scavenger hunt *plus* all the answers to every question in the quiz show yesterday."

"Are you kidding me?" Zoe asked, her jaw dropping.

132

"Where'd he get the envelope?"

My face warmed and I could feel my blood pumping faster. Wyatt *had* been cheating.

"No idea," Melvin said. "He could've gotten it from anywhere. He might've stolen it from someone. What I'm still confused about is how his team won the race on Tuesday. How'd he get to the finish line before everyone else?"

Zoe shook her head. "But his team hit the checkpoints. They got the apple from the baked beans and shaved the balloon! So Wyatt *was* in it."

"Funny thing is," Melvin said, "when I asked around, nobody actually saw Wyatt finish those challenges. And with a bunch of red ninjas on his team, it's not crazy to think the guys standing at those checkpoints just did them when no one was looking."

"That kind of explains how Wyatt got to the finish line early," I said. "I mean, he had enough time to pour himself a bowl of cereal before I got there."

"What?" Zoe asked, confused. "Cereal?"

"That Cookie Dough Delight stuff," I said. "So gross, but it's trending so everyone pretends to love it."

"No way…" Zoe whispered, staring at nothing. "*No way!*"

Melvin snapped his fingers. "That's the same cereal the student council room has, ain't it?"

"Ummm…" I hummed, still not connecting the same dots that Melvin and Zoe were.

"Do you know where the student council room is?" Zoe asked with a smirk. "Right around the corner from the finish line, down the narrow hall that everyone had to pass through at the end."

"Wyatt must've used that room to cut through as a shortcut!" Melvin said. "He probably poured himself a bowl of cereal since he had plenty of time to kill!"

"And he stole the envelope while he was in there?" I asked.

Zoe shook her head. "No, besides staff, there are only a couple of kids who have a key to get into that locked room. And they're both in student council."

"Whoa," I said, looking at Melvin. And then I whispered quietly while covering my mouth so Zoe couldn't read my lips.

133

"You think it was *my cousin* who helped Wyatt?"

"No, you dolt!" Melvin said.

"I was kidding!" I said, bumping my head with my palm. "If it was someone on student council, then my bet's on Colin. Somethin' about that kid has been on my radar since I first met him on Monday."

"No," Zoe said softly. "Colin and Bounty *don't* have keys. It's just me and the secretary…"

"What?" I asked, suddenly remembering who the secretary was. "That can't be right. The student council secretary? But that's—"

At that moment, the shadow of one of the red ninjas fell over us. It was the ninja that had ordered Melvin to stay in the room earlier, the girl ninja. The other two were still peeking their heads out the door, telling muffled jokes back and forth to each other.

I expected the red ninja to tell us to keep quiet, but she didn't. Instead, she pulled her mask up, just enough to expose her face.

It was Dani, the student council secretary.

"OMG," I whispered, utterly floored by the fact that Brayden's crush was a member of Wyatt's red ninja clan.

Dani opened her mouth, and then paused. At first I thought she was angry that we were onto her. But she wasn't. She was afraid. Frantic, even. "Please don't tell Brayden! Please! It all started as a ploy, but I actually think Brayden's super cool! And cute, but whatever! Just please don't tell him!"

"Bros got a code, sister," I said.

"I know, I know!" Dani whispered back. "But what I'm asking you to do is… *forget* about the code? Please! I'll do anything!"

Melvin leaned back and whistled.

"So that day in the hallway," I said. "When you were outside the men's restroom…"

"If you would'a gotten there five seconds sooner," Dani said, "you would've seen me push that envelope under the bathroom door. I'm the one who gave it to Wyatt."

Right at that second, we heard a loud *"POOF!"* come from the front of the room.

The doorway quickly filled with chalk dust so thick that it looked like a snowstorm. Maybe that was the advantage of wearing white ninja robes.

DANI!

MY FACE

Dani pulled her mask down again.

It was like someone opened the window at a chalk factory on a windy day. Within seconds, I couldn't see my hands in front of my face. I felt sorry for whoever the teacher was that used that classroom. It was *definitely* going to look like a white Christmas once the dust settled.

Suddenly I felt two hands grab at my arms, pulling me backward. I heard Zoe and Melvin grunt. The same thing must have happened to them, but there was no way I could tell from all the dust.

Was it The Scavengers again? Who else hated me in this school? Oh right, *everyone*.

I heard the red ninjas shout back and forth to each other.

Dani's voice was in the mix.

"What's going on?"

"Watch the door! It's gotta be his ninja clan!"

"Impossible! He doesn't even have a clan, does he?"

"Something touched my leg! SOMETHING TOUCHED MY LEG!"

The kid dragging me across the floor lifted me into one of the closets along the wall. We went from complete white out conditions to pitch black so my eyes were having a hard time adjusting.

The closet slipped shut quietly as the red ninjas continued panicking in the room.

"They're gone!"

"Cheesy rice! Wyatt's gonna blow a fuse!"

"We gotta find Chase before he gets to the gym! Come on!"

The door to the classroom slammed shut, and then it was silent.

In the dark closet, I heard the shuffling of feet and some whispers.

"Are they gone?" Zoe's voice whispered.

"Yepper pepper," said a boy's voice.

"Yepper pepper?" I repeated. "Slug?"

"Yepper pepper!" Slug replied.

Then came Gidget's voice. "Alright, dudes. Seriously, quit sayin' that."

Faith's voice came from farther down the closet. "OMG, I'm gonna freak out if I don't get out of here. Move it, people!"

The closet door swung open, and we all poured out onto the carpet. The room still had a light cloud of chalk dust drifting through the air.

I stood up, looking at our rescuers. It was Faith, along with Gidget and Slug.

"What're you guys doing here?" I asked, looking at the twins.

Gidget was the first to answer, even though she was already staring at her cellphone. "Meh," she said, like it was nothing. "Faith changed our minds about you."

"Changed your minds?"

"Yep!" Slug said with a goofy grin. "We're totally ninjas

now. I mean, we're in your ninja clan. That is, if you'll still have us."

I didn't know what to say. "But… you all quit," I said. "All three of you, including Melvin, decided that it wasn't your gig."

"Right," Gidget sighed. "And Faith changed our minds."

Faith stared at me like I was just supposed to get it.

"But—" I began.

Gidget spoke before I could get another word out. "Look, dude. You're way more awesome than you give yourself credit for. Faith helped us understand what being a good leader means, but more importantly, you *showed* us what it means."

Slug nodded, but said nothing.

Gidget lowered the phone and looked me right in the eye. "You might *not* be a good teacher, and by that I mean, a really *awful* teacher. I mean, just the *worst*."

Faith folded her arms. "Not helping."

137

"Right," Gidget said. "Anyway, you lead by example, which in my opinion, is the best kind of leader. You keep going, even when you can easily quit. You never give up. You might be a terrible teacher, but you're actually an *amazing* leader. You choose to do the right thing every time, even when it's uncool."

I looked at Faith. "Being a good leader doesn't mean the same thing as being a good teacher," I said, repeating what she had told me earlier in the week, finally understanding.

Faith nodded. "Your old ninja clan shouldn't have been your ninja clan. They were just leftover members from when Wyatt led the clan. It's time to rebuild the right way."

"With us," Slug said proudly.

For the first time in two weeks, I felt my heart swell. Goosebumps appeared on my forearms. It was like I was coming back to life. If I were in a movie, the sun would shine on my face as my black and white world filled with color. I never felt more awesome in my life. It was like finding out I was "the one."

"Guys," I said. "I don't know what to say."

"Then don't say anything," Faith said, slugging me in the arm.

I clutched at the spot she punched. "Wait!" I said, looking at Faith. "You're the white ninja!"

"Duh!" Faith said. "I thought we went over that last week! Remember? I said 'you're not the only one with secrets,' and you were all like 'blah blah blah blah' and stuff."

I shook my head. "Girls can be confusing sometimes."

"It's only gonna get worse as you get older," Zoe joked.

"Let's finish this," Melvin said. "I got the proof that Wyatt cheated. All you have to do is get it to Principal Davis."

"Who's in the gymnasium even as we speak," Zoe said.

I grabbed the envelope from Melvin's hands. "On it!"

Faith, Zoe, and I ran to the door and checked the hallway for red ninjas. It was all clear. And then, as if our lives depended on it, we all raced to the assembly.

Friday. 12:30 PM. The gymnasium.

Principal Davis sighed heavily into the microphone when Faith and I finally made it to the gym. "I guess this means Chase's team forfeits. Wyatt, it looks like—"

"Wait!" I shouted, running to the center of the gym. "We're here! We're both here!"

Faith huffed and puffed behind me, catching her breath.

All the sixth graders were already in the bleachers, bored and annoyed by the fact that they'd been waiting for close to thirty minutes.

Wyatt and his team were already at the center of the gym. When he saw the crinkled yellow envelope in my hand, his face turned white. He knew exactly what it was.

"Cutting it pretty close, don't you think, Mr. Cooper?" Principal Davis asked into the microphone from the front of the gymnasium.

I nodded, raising the envelope in my right hand, while clutching at a cramp in my side with my left hand. "Sorry," I said. "I have—"

"Of course," Wyatt said, just loud enough to cut me off. "Of course you can't beat me. You've *never* been able to beat me."

I stopped in place, listening to Wyatt's monologue.

"Remember your first week here?" he asked quietly as he

139

came closer. "I kicked your butt, man. And I could do it again and again, but you're too much of a goody-goody to take me on. Go ahead and tell on me, dude. *That's* why you've lost your ninja clan. *That's* why you're a lame-o leader – because you keep crying to someone else in charge."

My jaw was beginning to twitch. I could tell because my teeth were starting to hurt from how hard I was grinding them together.

"The principal's right there," Wyatt growled. "Your team didn't stand a chance against me and my red ninjas anyway. Dodge ball is a man's game."

Looking at the red dodge balls on the floor, I lowered the envelope.

"What're you doing?" Faith asked.

"Leading by example," I replied, turning away from the principal.

Once Faith and I met with Brayden and Gavin, the principal spoke into the mic again. "Five minutes to prep. After that the game begins."

"Why didn't you go to Principal Davis?" Faith asked.

"What's she talking about?" Brayden said.

I looked at Brayden, remembering that Dani wasn't who he thought she was. "I have proof that Wyatt cheated all week."

"Oh," Gavin said. "That's awesome, right? That means we win, doesn't it?"

I shook my head. "It does, but that's not how I want to win. Let's show Wyatt what we're made of for once. I'm tired of getting walked all over. No fists, no fighting, no trouble. Just an honest game of dodge ball. We can *win* this."

After a moment of looking at each other, my friends all agreed with me.

We were about to play the most important game of dodge ball we'd ever played in our lives.

And in front of the entire sixth grade class of Buchanan School.

No pressure, right?

Friday. 12:35 PM. Dodge ball.

Coach Cooper blew the whistle, starting the game.

Wyatt's team sprinted toward the red rubber balls sitting in a line at the center of the gym. My team was racing toward the same goal.

Our shoes squeaked loudly on the freshly polished floor, but the noise was mostly drowned out by the screaming kids in the bleachers.

Wyatt's team was faster, and made it to the dodge balls way before anyone on my team did.

Launching dodge balls straight for us, we all dove out of the way, avoiding the first wave of attack.

Rolling across the floor, I had to slide my body quickly to avoid a couple more balls that were thrown at me. Wyatt must've given the order to take me out first.

I saw Faith slide on her knees, grabbing a red ball and bringing it to her face to deflect one that Wyatt had thrown at her. It bounced off her ball, making the classic "PONG" sound that every sixth grader is familiar with.

Faith did a backwards somersault to get back to her feet. Then she clutched the ball with her right hand and swung it around once in a huge circle, flinging it across the gym like she was pitching a softball.

141

A kid from Wyatt's team tried catching the ball so Faith would get out, but she had thrown it too hard. It bounced off his hands and flew into some kids in the crowd.

"Out!" Coach Cooper shouted after blowing into his whistle.

Faith fist pumped while jumping up and down. She looked at me, excited to have the first out.

Suddenly, a red ball nailed her square in the cheek.

"No!" I shouted, reaching my hand out.

Stumbling back, Faith rubbed her cheek, but had a smile on her face. She rolled her eyes and shook her head like she was more embarrassed than upset. "Serves me right!" she yelled.

Brayden and Gavin were taking quick steps to the center line, their fingers gripping their dodge balls.

Gavin went with a simple overhanded approached to

throwing. His ball sailed a little too high, missing his target.

Brayden threw his arm out wide, sending his ball toward the ground. His strategy was to try and throw it low enough that it was impossible to catch, hitting the target just before bouncing on the floor. If you weren't paying attention, his ball would hit you, but if you saw it coming, all you had to do was lift a leg, allowing the ball to bounce away from you.

That's exactly what Wyatt did. He stepped forward, over Brayden's ball, like it was no big deal. Whipping both hands over his head, he chucked a dodge ball back at Brayden.

My best friend stepped backward to get out of the way, but caught his shoe on the floor. He fell to his butt as Wyatt's ball soared over his head, missing him.

It would've been a victory for Brayden except the rest of Wyatt's team noticed he was helpless on the ground.

Wyatt and the two kids on his team concentrated all their fire on Brayden. It was like a rapid-fire dodge ball machine, all aimed at one kid.

BRAYDEN'S FINAL MOMENTS...
IN THE GAME.

Brayden froze up, cowering on the floor as dodge balls rained down upon him. He never even had a chance.

The whistle was blown again. "Out!" Coach Cooper shouted, pointing at Brayden.

A few mumbles came from the crowd, but so did a few cheers. Wyatt, being the leader of the red ninjas, was sure to have fans watching.

"Down to you and me," Gavin said.

"If we can catch one of their balls, we can bring someone else back in," I said.

"But that's a bit risky."

"It is, but worth it if we can pull it off."

Gavin nodded, and sprinted toward the center line of the gym.

"Wait!" I said. "I didn't mean to *try* and get them to hit you!"

Gavin slid to a stop, bouncing on one foot, waving his arms around to keep from tripping.

Wyatt's team grabbed the dodge balls on the floor. They each took a few steps toward Gavin and then shot their dodge balls at him.

Gavin was impressive. He sidestepped the first few balls. They were coming at him too fast to try and catch. Grabbing a stray ball off the floor, Gavin pulled it up, barely able to block another ball from hitting him.

Chucking the ball at Wyatt, Gavin continued to taunt the opposite team by running back and forth along the center line.

I ran zigzagged toward Gavin as balls bounced past me. I kept reaching my hand out to catch one, but would shy away at the last second.

When I picked up a ball, I raised it over my head, looking at Wyatt. He was crawling along the floor reaching for his own dodge ball.

Throwing it with all my strength, the ball sailed through the air at the leader of the red ninjas.

Wyatt looked up. Instantly, he dropped his body to the floor, avoiding the dodge ball by millimeters.

Scooping up a ball of his own, Wyatt twisted his legs out and jumped off the floor like some kind of snake.

"Out!" Coach Cooper shouted again, pointing at one kid on Wyatt's team.

Gavin had his fist in the air. "Boom!" he said, and then pointed at the kid.

There were only four kids left in the middle of the gym. Everyone in the bleachers had gotten to their feet, shouting different cheers you'd hear at a basketball game.

The other boy on Wyatt's team was sprinting toward me with his dodge ball drawn back over his shoulder. He surprised me, which made me freeze up when he threw the ball at me.

Raising my arms instead of diving, the ball hit me right on my shoulder. I heard Wyatt laugh as I shuffled my feet backward.

Coach Cooper blew the whistle, and I took a breath as I started my walk to the side of the gym with Faith and Brayden.

"Over the line!" Coach Cooper shouted, pointing at the feet of the kid who had gotten me out. "You're out! Chase, *you're* still in!"

"Come on!" Wyatt shouted, holding his open palms out at the kid who was off sides.

Faith screamed excitedly, jumping up and down as Brayden shouted from the bench.

The coach pointed at me. "Get back in there," he ordered.

I spun around and jogged back toward Gavin who had his hand in the air, waiting to give me a high-five.

Suddenly, Gavin buckled to his feet as a "*PONG!*" echoed across the room. A red dodge ball rolled out from behind him. Gavin dropped to his knees and fell flat on his face as Wyatt stood at the center line.

Gavin groaned in pain as he rolled to his back.

"Out!" Coach Cooper shouted again, pointing to Gavin.

"I know, I know," Gavin said, pulling himself up. He made his trek to the bench that Faith and Brayden were at.

The entire crowd was going crazy. I couldn't tell if they were cheering for Wyatt or me, or if they were just screaming to make noise.

It was down to Wyatt and me. I wondered what the loading screen would look like at that moment if my life were a video game. It would probably be a picture of me next to a "versus" sign that Wyatt would be on the other side of.

PLAYER 1

PLAYER 2

VS

CHASE VS WYATT

SKILLS: NAPPING
QUOTE: "What? Napping
is so a skill."

SKILLS: ALL THE MARTIAL ARTS
QUOTE: "I'm awesome, and
you can quote me on that."

Taking a ball off the floor, I stepped toward the center line where Wyatt was already standing with his own ball. I flinched because on Wyatt's dodge ball was my name written in black marker. I don't know when he had the time to scribble it out, but I didn't care. I was more concerned about the fact that he did it at all. IMHO, that was a whole new level of pscyho that I wasn't comfortable dealing with.

"Looks like it's just you and me," Wyatt said, making sure my name was pointing at me on his dodge ball.

I nodded once. "Looks like."

"You won several small battles," Wyatt said. "But you're losing the war. You know that, right?"

I remained silent.

Everyone was still cheering as the two of us stood at the center of the gym, simply talking to each other.

"I know all about you and Naomi," Wyatt said suddenly.

146

Mentioning Naomi was like a punch to the gut. I had to blink rapidly to keep focus. "What about her?"

"You really stirred the pot with The Scavengers," Wyatt said, rolling his dodge ball in his hands.

"You know about The Scavengers?"

"I do *now*," Wyatt said with an evil grin. "Thanks to you."

"What's that supposed to mean?"

"Let's just say, Naomi and I have similar interests."

The crowd grew impatient, chanting in unison. "Hur-ry up! Hur-ry up! Hur-ry up!"

Wyatt took a step back, clutching his dodge ball as he did.

"*What's that mean?*" I shouted, not caring if anyone in the gym heard me.

Wyatt glanced to the side of the large room.

Naomi was against the wall with her arms folded, watching the game from the side of the gym.

I felt my knees grow weak.

At that instant, Wyatt's dodge ball said hello to the side of my face.

In dodge ball, the word for "hello" is "*PONG!*" along with a searing pain. I wouldn't recommend visiting the land of dodge ball. Tis a silly place.

Time slowed to a crawl as my brain tried to understand what was happening.

I was out.

I had just lost the only game I wasn't allowed to lose that week.

Everything happened in the blink of an eye. My world turned bright red and smelled like dirty rubber. The flash of red turned to white that faded slowly as I stumbled backward.

Wyatt had won. He beat me. Not fairly *or* squarely, but he *beat* me.

My cheek was on fire as the world spun circles. I saw the frozen faces of every sixth grader at Buchanan gasp in horror at how hard Wyatt had chucked the ball at me. Even Coach Cooper flinched with his hand over his mouth.

Losing my balance, I tripped over my feet, falling backward to the floor. Wyatt's ball seemed to hover over me. I must've jerked my face at the very last second, which bounced the ball straight over my head. It floated in the air as if someone had pushed the pause button.

Wyatt was patting his hands together like he had just finished a job well done.

Faith shouted my name from the side of the gym.

Brayden and Gavin were slouching on the bench, already looking defeated.

Naomi was still at the side of the bleachers. She was emotionless. Cold.

James Buchanan was dancing a jig and swinging in circles with a penguin in a tuxedo.

Okay, maybe that last thing was just in my head.

I landed on my butt with a whimper as the world started playing at normal speed again. The kids in the bleachers were so quiet that you could hear a bird fart.

And then I saw Gidget and Slug at the doors of the gym. The twins who quit my ninja clan, and then decided to stick around because they liked how I never give up.

…

148

I *never* give up.

I *couldn't* give up.

Even now.

Even when the dodge ball game seemed lost… I could still *win*.

Glancing up, I watched as gravity pulled Wyatt's ball back to the earth, but it wasn't directly over my head. When it said, *"PONG!"* to my face, it bounced off at a slight angle, and it had now started its descent. If that ball hit the ground, then the game really *would* be over.

I flipped to my stomach and launched myself across the polished floor, sliding to the spot where Wyatt's ball would land.

A gasp came from the crowd as I rolled to my back.

The ball landed perfectly in my hands.

"Ouuuuuuut!" Coach Cooper screamed in a high-pitched voice, pointing at Wyatt.

Everyone on the bleachers jumped to their feet, screaming cheers, but I couldn't hear any of it. My ears were still ringing from how high-pitched the coach's voice had been.

Even Miss Chen-Jung was celebrating at the back of the gym, waving her mop in the air, back and forth like it was a flag.

As I got to my feet, I saw Wyatt from the corner of my eye. He was jumping up and throwing a tantrum.

Faith smashed into me, giving me the biggest hug ever. Brayden and Gavin joined her, nearly knocking me to the floor. Everyone was there – even Zoe and Melvin had made it safely back to the gym.

Gavin rubbed his hand back and forth on top of my head. "That's how it's done!"

"*Boom!*" Brayden said, slugging my shoulder.

I was speechless as I clutched the dodge ball close to my stomach, afraid to drop it because I didn't want to take any chances. I once saw a football player drop the ball right before the end zone because they thought they were already in it. Because of that mistake, his team didn't get the touchdown and lost. I dug my fingers into the red rubber ball even tighter because I didn't want to make that same mistake.

"Are you alright?" Faith asked, looking at the death grip I had on the ball.

"Yeah, dude," Brayden joked. "What'd that ball ever do to you?"

Rubbing the ball burn on my cheek, I smiled.

"Oh, right," Brayden laughed. "It totally sucker punched you in the face."

"That ball hit you so hard that I bet your grandchildren felt it," Faith said. "Somewhere in the future, your grandson is holding his cheek, freaking out because it suddenly started stinging."

We all laughed.

Wyatt's voice sliced through the cheers and laughter. "That doesn't count!" he screamed.

I spun in place and saw the leader of the red ninja clan stomping across the gymnasium floor, straight for me. There was no way he'd try to start a fight in the middle of all the sixth graders? Was he that bold?

Good thing I didn't have to find out.

Principal Davis cut Wyatt off, stepping in front of him.

And guess what? Dani was right next to the principal. She

was already out of her red ninja robes and back in her street clothes.

"Guys, look," I said, pointing to the principal.

I couldn't hear what they were saying since the cheers from the crowd were still so loud. All I knew was Wyatt's eyes grew to the size of watermelons as his mouth moved quickly. He just kept shaking his head and making gestures at Dani.

Dani's face was stone cold. She stood with her arms crossed, rolling her eyes every couple seconds, and then saying something in response.

Brayden stopped behind me. "What's the deal? What's Dani doing out there?"

I'd forgotten that Brayden didn't know that Dani was a red ninja.

Principal Davis gestured to the side of the gym. Wyatt tried arguing again, but stopped once the principal started tapping his foot.

Dani kept her head down as the principal turned to her. She nodded slowly, and then looked up at me... no, she looked at Brayden.

Principal Davis looked back too, and then let his chest fall like he was sighing. He nodded at Dani, which was when she started jogging over to us.

"Dani," Brayden said. "What's going on? What just happened over there?"

Dani paused, with eyes soft and wet. "I'm sorry," she said with a quiver in her voice. "I haven't been honest with you."

"What are you talking about?"

"I was helping Wyatt this week," she said. "That's how he was winning."

Brayden's jaw dropped as he stared at her.

"But why?" Zoe asked, not angry, but genuinely curious.

Dani paused. "Because Wyatt offered me the lead position in the red ninja club he was going to start when he won. I was going to run the entire thing if I helped him. And I made the wrong choice, but…" she looked at Brayden. "I'm sorry. It was so dumb of me. I got greedy and slipped up."

Brayden remained silent.

"I made the wrong choice," Dani said again, "But I hope that doing the right thing in the end can make up for it? Or at least start to?" And then she looked at me. "Lead by example, right?"

I blinked. Dani was working with the bad guy this week. Some would even say that she *was* a bad guy, but what happens when a bad guy realizes they don't need to be that anymore?

Dani was suddenly the answer to that question. She took a stand and did what was right, even in front of her peers, and let's face it – there were *tons* of red ninjas watching from the bleachers. She didn't just stand up to Wyatt – she just stood up to *all* of them.

Which was probably why Brayden had a funny grin on his face.

"You just did the coolest thing I've ever seen anybody do," Brayden said at last.

Zoe nodded, and then spoke. "You can't be on the student council anymore."

"What?" Brayden cried. "Come on! She did the right thing!"

Dani grabbed Brayden's hand. "No," she said. "Zoe's right. I still have to pay for what I did, and I'll happily do it. I'll probably get detention or even suspended because of cheating, but I'm okay with it because I know I'll never do it again."

Man. Dani was awesome.

"You and your friends showed me that it's way cooler to be cool to everyone," she said, looking at all of us – Brayden, Zoe, Faith, Gavin, and me. "So I hope you guys don't hate me because I'd really like to be part of your group."

Brayden smiled at me. I knew exactly what he was thinking.

"Y'know," I said. "Word in the school is there's *another* ninja clan that's looking for new members. You might be exactly the kind of kid they're after."

Dani smiled with a twinkle in her eye. "But do you think I'm good enough for the white ninja clan?"

I stuttered. "I… no, I mean, not them… mine."

Dani laughed. "I'm kidding. I know what you meant."

"I bet if you volunteer to help with the Buchanan Bash next week," Zoe added, "I could get Principal Davis to reduce any kind of detention time you'll have."

"Cool," Dani said.

The ex-red ninja turned around and rejoined Principal Davis. Together, they walked out of the gym.

Wyatt was at the door, waiting for the principal to come get him, but he wasn't alone. He was leaning against the walls, engaged in conversation with another girl.

It was Naomi.

I didn't know what they were talking about, but I knew it had something to do with me because every couple seconds, Wyatt would look across the room at me.

What do you get when you mix Wyatt and the red ninja clan with The Scavengers?

Trouble.

I spun around to face the spot on the bleachers where my friends were sitting, but something else caught my eye. At the far end of the gym, opposite of where Wyatt and Naomi were, I saw a shadowed figure near the exit. I only noticed him because the reflection in his glasses glinted at me.

Squinting, I tried to focus on the boy's face, but it was too dark to make out anything except for his glasses and a small white square on his shirt.

The longer I stared, the more clear the square became…

The square on his shirt... I think that it read…

Victor. Great.

I looked away immediately because I couldn't tell if Victor was looking at me or not. But whatever. It was something I didn't need to deal with that day, or hopefully ever.

Once the crowd calmed down, Zoe took the microphone and officially announced that my team had won the games for the Spirit Week. She went on to explain a little bit about the club I wanted to start – the one with the candy bar.

I took a seat on one of the bleachers at the side of the gym. Faith joined me.

"What's up?" she asked. "What're you thinking?"

I took a deep breath, realizing I had actually been holding it in. "Nothing," I said, smiling. To my surprise, my smile *wasn't* fake.

I wasn't sure what was in store for my future. The Scavengers weren't finished with me, that much was clear. Wyatt and his red ninjas were still growing. Jake had a chip on his shoulder about me and was also a member of the Scavengers now. And some eighth grade Scavenger named Victor had just joined the Chase Haters Club.

But I was still smiling.

"Nothing's up," I said, looking at Faith.

"You're not in this alone," Faith said as if she could read my mind.

I nodded. "I know. It's good to know I have a friend… and a white ninja that has my back."

Faith knew I knew, but she still blushed.

"You're gonna have to tell me all about it," I said with a smirk.

"I will," she said. "But it can wait. Right now, you have a victory to celebrate and a new club to start."

Zoe wrapped up on the mic. All the sixth graders were allowed to leave their seats and hang out on the gymnasium floor until the bell rang.

Instead of getting up and walking around, I decided to sit and watch everyone carry on with their lives as if nothing was wrong – as if Buchanan School didn't hold terrifying secrets that would rock them to their core if they had any idea.

Faith pulled out her cellphone and brought up the camera.

155

She leaned closer, holding her phone out in front of both of us.

I made a dorky face.

Faith paused, lowering her phone. "Can you just take a normal picture for once?"

"Uh, yeah," I said. "Sorry. Go ahead."

Lifting the camera up again, Faith snapped a selfie. "Did you make a dumb face?"

"No!" I said right away.

"If you did, I'm posting it online," she joked.

Faith stayed by my side for the rest of the assembly. She didn't say anything else, but she didn't need to.

After all, best friends are the ones who can just hang out and be real without having to say a word.

Stories – what an incredible way to open one's mind to a fantastic world of adventure. It's my hope that this story has inspired you in some way, lighting a fire that maybe you didn't know you had. Keep that flame burning no matter what. It represents your sense of adventure and creativity, and that's something nobody can take from you. Thanks for reading! If you enjoyed this book, I ask that you help spread the word by sharing it or leaving an honest review!

- Marcus
m@MarcusEmerson.com

IF YOU LIKE CHASE COOPER'S STORY,
THEN YOU'LL LOVE THE STORY ABOUT
HIS GREAT-GREAT-GRANDSON.

MIDDLE SCHOOL NINJA
IS AVAILABLE NOW!

Made in the USA
Middletown, DE
20 May 2021